NEW YORK MADNESS

HERE's Maxwell Bodenheim's biggest book about fast, modern life in New York—the novel for which *Georgie May, Replenishing Jessica* and *Ninth Avenue* were only a preparation.

It's the story of two bright, vivacious New York girls, game and scrappy kids full of youth's zest for life, and willing to go anywhere, try anything to satisfy their fierce craving for excitement. Their quest leads them to New York's toughest spots, the East Side, the Far West of gangland and the waterfront dives, the Spanish Section, Union Square with its fearless and desperate radicals, and the racketeer hells on the Broadway side streets. Their adventures and their men make a story of enthralling power; and their discovery of the only way to get clear of New York Madness brings it to a climax of terrific punch.

Bodenheim has never written a more glamorous, sweeping story, reflecting sophisticate New York's own racy lingo.

BOOKS BY MAXWELL BODENHEIM

Minna and Myself, poetry (1918)
Advice: a book of poems, poetry (1920)
Introducing Irony, poetry (1922)
Against This Age, poetry (1923)
Blackguard, novel (1923)
The Sardonic Arm, poetry (1923)
Crazy Man, novel (1924)
Cutie: A Warm Mamma, short story (with Ben Hecht, 1924)
Replenishing Jessica, novel (1925)
Ninth Avenue, novel (1926)
Returning to Emotion, poetry (1927)
Georgie May, novel (1928)
The King of Spain, poetry (1928)
Sixty Seconds, novel (1929)
Bringing Jazz!, poetry (1930)
Naked on Roller Skates, novel (1930)
A Virtuous Girl, novel (1930)
Duke Herring, novel (1931)
Run, Sheep, Run, novel (1932)
Six A.M., novel (1932)
New York Madness, novel (1933)
Slow Vision, novel (1933)
Lights in the Valley, poetry (1942)
Selected Poems, poetry (1946)

"His is a bold and free interpretation of American life. . . . *New York Madness* does not deal with the silk-hatted and Paris gowned set, but with the girls and men of the seven million who live and love, told largely in their own racy lingo. It is a cross section of metropolitan life. Maxwell Bodenheim's followers are certain to welcome it."
Dayton Daily News, January 26, 1934

"It is obvious that the author had difficulty keeping his talents as a propagandist subjugated, but none the less he has succeeded, and the story, daring and sordid as it is, has color, vigor and force."
The New Books in Review, September 23, 1933

"He has overtaken Honoré Balzac at last and is now treading on the heels of Guy de Maupassant. . . . Bodenheim has his district dead to rights."
Brooklyn Daily Eagle, August 30, 1933

"If you like 'naughty' books, then *New York Madness* with its story of two rather sleazy young women and their experiences with their boy friends will give you your money's worth. That's precisely what the author intended. . . . In a sense, this book is something of an object lesson. It neither is nor is not pornographic. To those who prefer their erotics straight, it will be as unsatisfactory as it will be to the prudes."
Richmond Times-Dispatch, September 3, 1933

"Gay gals and tough gents scurry through this new book by Maxwell Bodenheim in search of what they take to be 'life,' and the study of their antics makes absorbing reading under the author's inspired guidance.... As in all of Mr. Bodenheim's novels, he is frank in his dealings with the tangled situations which arise, and timorous readers may as well pass the volume by. They might not share the author's enthusiasm for unvarnished narrative concerning the lives of those who fill the pages of *New York Madness*."
THE ATLANTA JOURNAL, SEPTEMBER 10, 1933

"In these torrid adventures of Alicia in Gangland and Mona in Bohemia, you are presented with Mr. Bodenheim's mad metropolis as setting for a variety of erotic episodes and quaint sentimentalities.... Obviously, this is not a book for children; nor, for that matter, for adults."
THE LOS ANGELES TIMES, SEPTEMBER 24, 1933

"The book is sordid but well written. The characterization, conversation and incidents all blend smoothly into the murky background of night life among the lower class of New Yorkers. Bodenheim writes consistently and with that daring which stories of the exposé type require. A story such as this might advisably display a 'Minors not admitted' placard, but those who have reached the age of indiscretion might profit by its revelation of the low wages of sin."
THE OREGON DAILY JOURNAL, SEPTEMBER 10, 1933

"If the life of the denizens of New York's average apartments is as vicious and as hard as Maxwell Bodenheim would have you believe in *New York Madness*, thank Heaven for the great northwest.... It's exceedingly disgusting in places—too many places—and it's far from convincing."
THE MINNEAPOLIS STAR, AUGUST 24, 1933

―――――

"Few persons know New York as Maxwell Bodenheim and few who do write about it with his flair for color and sensation. His New York is raw and realistic. It's this New York of strange colors and strange people, brilliance, sophistication, boldness, racketeering, dancing, recklessness that serves as the background for this new novel."
THE SUNDAY OREGONIAN, OCTOBER 8, 1933

―――――

"Maxwell Bodenheim to me is the most objectionable writer living."
THE WORLD AND ALL, SEPTEMBER 9, 1933

Copyright © 1933 by The Macaulay Company

ISBN 979-8-218-54828-5

This edition published in 2025 by
Tough Poets Press
Arlington, Massachusetts 02476
U.S.A.

www.toughpoets.com

NEW YORK MADNESS

Maxwell Bodenheim

Tough Poets Press
Arlington, Massachusetts

Chapter One

ALICIA MCCULLEY was bored, mournful, even gangrenous, but in every accidental collision between these conditions, each one became less convinced of its reality and strove to strengthen itself in the confusion of mutual insult. Such entanglements, branching from the elaborate misunderstandings between spirit and sexual organs, are always trivialities in the estimation of the militantly cultured, seriously redundant, robust apostles of sanity who infest every land and generation; but Alicia was only slightly affected and, mercifully, not quite sane. She sprawled on the bed-couch in her room and one of her long, subtly half-slender legs made the letter V as the heel of one foot touched the knee of the other leg. She was naked. The summer night angered her, took on the guise of a limp, almost impersonal lover who refused to be dismissed. Her mind was disjointed as it gave battle to a few among the horde of civilized deceits around her.

"He couldn't keep his fingers from sliding—oh, ever so slightly—into the side of my breast when we were dancing. I'd have a thousand times more respect for any man if he'd lift my dress and kiss my legs, right on the dance-floor, and then he could say: 'Let's stand on our heads and nibble watermelon rind. Let's kneel down and hug in time to the music, or let's tie our waists together, with my coat or your dress, and dance that way.' Anything that would be beautiful, impulsive nonsense and to hell with all these habits, *habits*. The bouncer would rush up and smack him down, and the cops would pinch him, and the people in the ballroom, wouldn't they joke and sneer about it? Wouldn't they?

"Oh, well, everything goes if it's on the sly. Otherwise, it's broccoli and calomel and the nervous, self-conscious dears can't stand it—not before the fifth drink anyway. Refined people are bored to death with themselves, at least half of the time—isn't it a fact? Maybe that's why they find it so hard to be indifferent, or tolerant, to people who aren't refined. I can't hear a sound from the alcove. Mona must be falling asleep. In a few minutes she'll be wheezing and purring, like grandmother's carpet-sweeper. Cheaper, sweeper, cheaper in a good old way. The kid ought to have her nose operated on, but where in hell will she ever get the money? She can't even spare the time off from her job. Money! I love it and I hate it. Didn't the ostrich have a bad smell, lady? Maybe that's why he was 'ostrichized.' Oh, my dear, you're so cheap and childlike when you're . . . just trying to be shocking. I've got a better idea—sell wrapping-paper and cotton gladiolas at Woolworth's instead, or buy a nice mink coat and walk down all the streets, so you won't freeze to death while you're hunting for something beautiful."

Alicia turned to the book which she had been reading—*The Roumanian*, by Tyrus Thaine. The book was a best-seller and Alicia had waited three weeks to procure it from a circulating-library. She spat, pensively, on one of the pages and her thoughts rallied in the direction of words, which they could not quite find, words such as: "It's a best-seller because it's fizzy, clever, facetious, and, oh, hopelessly sophisticated about sex. If it was really in sympathy with underdogs and hell-raisers, with renegades and lonely souls, and if it took all of the smelly bluffs and made them parade nakedly down

Fifth Avenue, instead of playing parcheesi with them, I wouldn't have had to wait three weeks to get it, I'd have found it in a second-hand book store on Fourth Avenue, marked down to thirty cents."

Her thoughts became lazier, made fitful raids into the past. "I can't even remember that boy's name—he had bushy eyebrows and a loose mouth, and he was always asking me: 'Why don't you study sociology?' I'll never forget the night when he dragged me over to that place—The New School for Social Research. The lecturer had a face like cold lard with shoe-buckles for eyes, and the whole room seemed to have a dry smell to it—oh, tremendously educated, and uppish, and knowing . . . and I was sniffing like a pet terrier and the boy asked me, did I have a cold? They had a wrangle about economic exterminators . . . no, economic . . . determination. It made such a difference. They were all throwing long words at one another, but the words were acting like . . . like acrobats with stage-fright—aren't I smart?—and it took them one whole hour to call each other pie-faced liars, and I, little, insignificant me, got up and said that they could have done it in a much shorter time and then they could have adjourned to have a drink. The lecturer said I was wasting my time and ought to listen to what I was more naturally interested in—something like a row between a traffic cop and a hack driver. I think he said policeman—cop would have been too short a word for him. I invited him to come out with me and listen to the row himself—rub his nose on the street pavement, for a change—and the boy beside me begged me for God's sake to keep quiet and act decent. Then, afterwards, he walked me home, bawling me out every inch of the way, but when we were in my room, he finally forgot about sociology and tried to feel my legs on the couch. Even a highbrow must have his absent-minded moments . . ."

A noise pushed Alicia back to the immediate scene. Three raps, repeated twice, could be heard from the door beside the alcove.

"Who is it? Is it you, Joe?"

The raps came again, louder now.

"Who *is* it?"

The only answer was a reiterated knocking. Rising from the bed, Alicia hurried into magenta silk pajamas and black slippers, and approached the door. Her long, oval face was proudly indifferent, slightly inquisitive, and perturbed in the swiftness of a trivial indecision. Husky, subdued words floated from the hallway.

"I've got a message from Joe. Joe. He's in trouble. He wants you to help him."

Joe Rosenbaum was the owner of a speak-easy and the man whom Alicia loved. She knew only too well that his life frequently assumed the proportions of a miracle, scheming, placating and fighting its way through the ever-present gangsters, cops and drunks. Hideously worried now, she opened the door. A strange man, with his right elbow raised almost to his shoulder, made an eel-like motion and gained entrance to the room before Alicia could draw another breath. In a tan linen suit freshly pressed, a blue shirt and tie, mahogany shoes, and with his Panama held in his hand, the man looked like half a million others in New York City—hard-faced, galvanized apes with a twist of the veiledly unscrupulous around their tight mouths and using an immaculate front emblematic of the money for which they were constantly angling.

He walked to the center of the room and stood there, easily, with the manner of one who was paying an unexpected social visit. Remaining beside the partly open door, Alicia stared at him with anxiety and distrust.

"Well, what *is* the message, and *why* did you squirm in here without my asking you?"

Instead of answering, the man merely shifted his feet and gave her the hard symptom of a smile, in which he thumbed his nose at her without the actual, physical gesture. Angry and disbelieving now—angered also by her own credulous impulse—Alicia clenched one of her hands and her slim body vibrated, like the snapped end of a trolley wire.

"Why, of all the nerve! You get out of here—get out of here this instant!"

Stepping nearer, the man examined her with a mildly greasy, practical confidence, and within the unknown, stunted ravening of his heart and soul, he was bored and vicious without realizing the incongruity. He could not have been more than thirty and his eyes were pin-heads on both sides of a broken nose, and his brown hair, parted on the side, was thick with glostora.

"Oh, come on . . . you remember me. Sure you do. You were talking it over with me the other night down at Joe's place."

His voice sounded like a scratchy phonograph and he knew that inspiration and routine were not always enemies in their pursuit of small, material designs. Alicia suddenly realized that she was too tired to be indignant, that the conventions of fear and intactness, in a situation such as the present one, were burdensome and never quite sincere.

"*Are* you going to leave, or will I have to run down and call a cop?"

Silence.

"What on earth do you *want* of me? There isn't a single thing here worth stealing and it won't do you any good to jump on me. Are you drunk, or just plain crazy?"

The gentleman in tan became paternally wolfish, in a contrast which would not have existed, if it had paused in any effort to understand itself. In his duality of professional lover and exploiter, his emotions often barely relented, against their will, and his self-inspection was then not sufficiently alert to distinguish any difference between the two.

"Aw, listen, sweetness . . . you don't want to get nervous. It's all on the up and up—sure it is. I met you down at Joe's joint about a week ago—remember? You said you'd fix me up any time I dropped in on you."

"Oh, stop it. You're lying and you know you are. You've got some game, and you might as well come out with it. What is it?"

The man walked to a chair near the bed-couch and sat on the arm-rest, with one leg swinging to and fro, one finger balancing the Panama, and all of the motions executed with an ease and finality which transcended mere complacency and became meanly, menacingly inevitable—inevitable to Alicia too. She had the feeling that, beneath the minimum of illusory motion, this man's intentions were as fixed as shrivelled Buddhas still not quite visible to her eye, and, standing with one hand on the door-knob, she forgot for a moment that she was alive. She became, to herself, insignificant and unsubstantial in some pettily insistent trick of existence. A strong effort was needed to bring back the old, reliable formulas of cold amusement, wrathful intactness. What did any incident matter, beyond the false drama expended to make it indelible, important to itself? She took one step from the door, and halted.

"I'd love to accommodate you—you're such a quaint fool, aren't you?—but I don't know exactly what you're after. Am I expected to sit in your lap, or do you want to have a chat with me?"

The man slid down to the seat of the chair and, as he crossed his legs, he was dreamily casual and chop-licking, with a hint of secure insolence.

"Oh, be yourself, baby. You don't need to be afraid of me—I'm not a dick and I won't get you into any trouble. I was nuts about you the first time I met you—you're just the candy-box I'm looking for. How much are you going to tax me, sweetness?"

"*Tax* you?"

"Sure, you know what I mean. If you trim it down to five bucks, I'll bring you plenty of trade, baby."

After his last words, he observed her with an appearance of cursory expectation, which was hardly more personal than that which a man in a restaurant might have had, relaxing before the waitress busied herself to fill his order, though, inwardly, he was not without a sizable lust. His sensuality had graduated from a coarse school, where softness scarcely dared to manifest itself, lest it be ridiculed or annihilated. Between a persuasion of rage and flitting grimaces at the first emotion, Alicia hesitated. The man was equally comical and repugnant to her, and she could not decide upon a course of action. To cry for help seemed babyish and inadequate—an affront to her sense of adult resourcefulness—and, in addition, she had no desire to run down to the street and leave this man alone with Mona Farrideau, her apartment-mate, who slept always so soundly that something like a train wreck was needed to awaken her.

Retreating to the door, Alicia eyed her visitor with an icy, practical disgust and resolved to try dramatics, in the hope of frightening him.

"You've got the nerve of a brass rat—do you know that? Well, you have, and I'm going to rouse the whole house and have you arrested, if you don't leave the room this minute!"

The man sprang from the chair, and he had the face of one grinning darkly over some private joke. Certain that Alicia was not acting but was determined not to tolerate him, he extracted a vindictive relish from his subsequent actions and words. He spoke rapidly.

"It's a good act, babe, but you're not fooling anybody. I get the idea now. You're expecting some other guy and you're afraid I'll gum up the works, but don't worry, pie-face—I'll make it short and sweet. I'll dig up ten bucks too, ten smackos, just to show you what a good sport I am."

The turmoil commenced now—the agitation which was sordid only to the secret impotence of its aggressors, and to the invisible millions indirectly responsible for it. The man strode to the short mantelpiece beside the bed-couch and tucked a bill under a bluish green, Bohemian-glass vase. Then he turned and glided toward the alcove, where Mona was sleeping, and disappeared behind the red, cotton-brocade portières. He removed the bed-sheet from Mona and dropped his hands, heavily, on her naked breasts, but she only tossed from one side to another, without quite awakening.

Rattled and furious by turns, Alicia knew that he was attempting to draw her away from the safety of the door, but a sudden, wild desire to protect Mona overpowered this knowledge and she rushed into the alcove, to leap upon him. He dodged past her, with the uncanny side-twist of a professional acrobat and hurried to the door, clicking the catch which locked it from the outside. Then he ran to one of the front windows and jerked the cream shade up and down, twice. As Alicia sped from the alcove, she slipped on a small, gray rug, near the door, and fell to a sitting posture. It was one of those interventions of chance—impersonal jests or undivided laws—always ready to deride human will power, fatuousness. If she had been able to reach the hallway, she might have spoiled, or seriously disturbed, the plans of the man in the room, but now he was already rushing from the window and when she rose to her feet, rubbing the bruise on her knee, he caught and held her.

With the main part of his task accomplished, he decided to wrestle with her, as an urchin might worry a terrier, discontentedly, and to punish it for its aloofness. In spite of her kicks and scratches, he pulled her around the room, cuffing and pinching her face and body. The lip-smacking was partly unscrupulous and careless, to itself, but in the remainder of his motives he felt entirely justified. To his education and temperament, Alicia was neither blameless nor over-abused. He divided women into inflexible classes. Those in the first were impeccably respectable. They imbibed only occasionally and never beyond the second drink; they were ruled by solidly regular husbands, or relatives, and their inhibitions and modesties were never deserted to any appreciable extent.

The women in the second class were the ones who "took chances." They lived alone, or with a man to whom they were not married, and sometimes they allowed themselves to become perceptibly alcoholic in public places, and because they dared to desecrate the sacred conventions and restraints always assigned to their sex, they deserved to be ill-treated.

Similar to many small crooks and gangsters, the man in tan was a sightless Puritan at heart, and he selfishly honored his mother, his sisters, and would have fought to his death to protect them.

Alicia was almost insane with anger now, and with a clawing, kicking lunge she escaped her tormentor and ran toward the alcove. At that moment a pounding came from the door simultaneously with the appearance of Mona Farrideau.

Mona was stout, young, of medium height, with a thickly milky skin, a tremendous mop of golden hair, and a large, broadly modelled face, which had the suggestion of a lioness when it was fully aroused. Though her green eyes were still puffy and squinting with the remnants of sleep, they quickly contracted, became murderously cold and smoldering, as they peered at the man, who was eyeing her, in turn, with an intent, business-like surmise.

Holding the instinct, which so often rescues the essentially feeble minds of prescribed animals, he feared Mona much more than Alicia and felt himself in the presence of a more practical and yet savagely competent woman. The pounding had not relaxed. The man darted to the door, and as he did, Mona, who was standing some two feet away from it, struck him on the side of the head with her fist, as quickly as a lioness might sideswipe an over-close passer-by through the bars of a cage. Mona was unusually strong, for a woman, and the man stumbled and was forced into a jig-step to regain his balance. For a moment, he turned to retaliate, but changed his mind and fumbled with the lock on the door, as Mona hastened to Alicia. With arms interlocked, the two women glanced, alternately, from the doorway to each other, and Alicia's face, with its black eyes, long thin-tipped nose, and flexible mouth, was working through every expression of hatred and shame incredulously combined. She spoke quickly to Mona.

"They're going to frame us, say we take men for money."

"God, if I'd only woke up sooner! . . . What'll we *do*?"

"Oh, I wish I knew. It's an outrage. I should have called you before, but I thought I could handle it . . . couldn't get it into that thick head of mine!"

"Well, you stick with me, kid. There must be some way out of it."

The door had opened and a pair of newcomers confronted the girls. They were tall, with gargantuan shoulders, and black derbies were clamped insolently on their heads, and they wore dark suits, immaculate but slightly ill-fitting. One of them had a jaw like the angle of a cornice, a lumpy nose, and small, fishily appraising eyes, while the other's face was flabby, with a stub nose and the almost petulant lips of an overgrown, professional bad-boy not quite in love with his task. The man in tan stood beside a writing-table near the center of the room and pretended that he was downcast, nervous, chagrined—a ludicrous, transparent pretense.

The next few minutes resolved themselves into a painful, machine-like farce.

"Nice little flat. Been having a lot of parties like this?" The cornice-jawed one stepped nearer to the girls.

"Certainly not. What's the idea—what are you trying to put over?" Alicia was frightened but tried to inject snap into her voice.

The men extracted shields and waved them, negligently, before returning them to their coat-pockets.

"Don't get funny—we've been watching this flat for a week and we know plenty." The flabby-faced detective adopted his best glower and then continued the farce by cross-examining the man in tan.

"Did you pay anything to this jane?"

The accomplice simulated a modicum of reluctant oppression.

"Come on, spit it out before I take a sock at you. Did you pay her?"

"Yeah, I gave her a sawbuck."

"Which one?"

More silence.

"Clean your ears out, you mut. Which one was it?"

"Aw, the one in the red outfit."

The detective glanced behind him for a moment.

"The one with the lead-pencil legs, huh?"

"That's right, chief."

"How about the other baby?"

"Aw, she was willing enough but I'm no millionaire. I've got to go out and sweat for the coin I make."

"Where'd she put the money—did you notice?"

Silence again.

"Come on . . . come on. Talk up now . . . talk up, or I'll bust your nose in for you!"

"Aw, leave me alone . . . if you've got to know, she put it over there on the mantel under the blue jar."

The lumpy-nosed detective, Frank Stallings, walked to the mantel, retrieved the bill and tucked it into a vest-pocket, while his partner, Mike Conley, drew nearer to the girls and eyed their bodies, faces, with a rigidly bored and yet intent exhaustiveness, as though they were caged possessions and he was only passing through the familiar routine of ticketing and certifying them. Mona and Alicia felt a tawdry, ominous joke pulling their overwrought emotions, irresistibly, and, one by one, they rippled out in hysterical laughter, as they paced up and down before the bed-couch. The entire performance had been so crudely mundane that they could scarcely credit its reality, or effectiveness. Mona spoke to Alicia.

"Honest," this is positively the crudest performance I've ever seen."

"Of course. They know they don't have to be clever. If they get us into court they'll simply lie themselves blue in the face."

The man in tan had sneaked through the doorway and departed, while Stallings and Conley were pretending to be obliviously immersed in their search through the apartment. When her laughter died, Mona felt blasphemous and yet craftily alert, while Alicia was fighting off the desire to whimper, since her spirit was more complexly and sensitively adjusted than that of Mona—a difference which existed irrespective of the unreliable, grandstand myth called physical courage. Mona walked over to Stallings and spoke.

"Where are you taking us?"

"You know where—over to the women's hotel at Jefferson Market."

"How much money are you after?"

Stallings showed a faint, rancid grin.

"Trying to bribe an officer, huh? Well, I want a million bucks, girlie . . . and don't make me laugh. You put some clothes over that fat can of yours and you trot along with me, or I'll whale you where you won't like it."

Alicia approached Mona and tugged at her sleeve.

"Darling, don't . . . it's impossible. They're too dirty clever to commit themselves now. They'll work it on the sly, I know."

Mona ignored Alicia and still looked at Stallings. Suddenly, she felt humiliated—small, stupid and prostrate. The masochism gathered in strength and told her that she would be justified in using any expedient that could placate the two apes in black derbies and send them alone into the night, and in this respect, the gift of her body seemed to be no more than stoical triviality. Her broad face with its high cheek-bones and wide mouth was a study in repugnance and enforced ogling insidiously accepting one another, and she had the mood of an actress, gayly, nauseatedly, urging herself toward an inevitable sacrifice written into the play by another self within her.

"See here, you big slob . . . why can't you be reasonable?"

"Reas'nable? . . . What are you driving at?"

"Listen, the whole thing's a dirty frame-up and you know it, but we can't prove anything and you've got us just where you want us. If you promise not to arrest us and you'll leave us alone afterwards . . . well, I'll do something for you, but you've got to make it quick and then leave us alone. It's up to you."

As Stallings looked at Mona, he had the contempt of one who hated both the alleged inferiority of women and the power of this inferiority to control and softly disarm him for a time. His hardness, like that of many other men of his rank and stratum, continually exaggerated itself to escape being rendered extinct by the hardness of other men and to conceal the few, relenting crinkles which even his environments had been unable quite to dispel. He drove one of his palms, playfully, against Mona's shoulder.

"All right, baby . . . it's a go. You're a fat, sweet article . . . don't ever fool yourself about that. You're sweet 'n' high class, kid."

He pinched her cheeks, stroked her shoulders and breasts, with remarkably delicate hands, his face still surly. He was a rough-neck lulled to sleep by the oblique pipings of sex, and yet not entirely, with over one-half of him still a restive audience. Alicia jerked Mona around, savagely.

"Mona . . . are you out of your head?"

"Not more than usual."

"Oh, Mona . . . please . . . it's all a joke and you've got to forget about it. This man wouldn't keep his promise no matter what you did. He'd laugh in your face the very minute it was over! I know he would."

Mona knew that Alicia was undoubtedly right, but she could not immediately check the counter-impulses—the carelessly self-lowered feeling, and the fear of a jail-cell, a calloused, inattentive judge. Stallings, still caressing Mona's breast, gave a twist of his eye to Conley—a signal for the latter to approach and drag Alicia away. At this moment, knuckles sounded again on the door-panels—three raps, one long and two short. Alicia hugged Mona, despairingly, while the detectives walked to the door and opened it.

The man standing in the hallway was a bit over medium height, with a broad torso, comparatively narrower legs, and a sallow, brown-eyed, hook-nosed face—a face where soft and rasping characteristics were unobtrusive, mutually friendly in the habits of a hard tolerance created by years of adaptation to polite and violent extremes of environment. Twirling the sacred, black derby—the crown of eternal, bluntly aggressive smugness—Stallings scanned the newcomer with a heavy weave of indifference and satisfaction, too over-worked, in such situations, to be much interested in proximities and their cut-and-dried results.

"Oh, uh . . . hello, Joe. How's the boy?"

"Not so bad."

"That's fine. Come to see your girl-friend, I suppose."

"Well, yes . . . but not with your number elevens planted in the doorway, Frank. What's going on here—what's the trouble?"

"Oh, nothing much. We're just trotting her over to the Market on a charge of prostitution. She's been starting a little collection-agency on the side, the poor kid."

Conley talked over the shoulder of Stallings.

"Sure, that's all it was—just picking up some easy change with the fat blonde she's chumming with. But say, what's the matter, Joe? Can't you slip her enough cash yourself?"

Joe Rosenbaum became angry under the thrusts of this vicious kidding, but the anger died almost instantly. He had schooled himself to step, automatically, from the pathways of steam-rollers, when the identities were unmistakable, and a long experience with the evasively brutal, ever-minimized averages of life in New York City had persuaded him to repress, or conceal, most of his originally hot-blooded aversions and encourage only those not confronted by any threat of extinction under unfair odds.

Alicia and Mona were huddled together, a few paces behind the detectives, and Alicia cried out: "Joe, Joe! . . . come inside, please! I've *got* to talk to you. It's all a dirty, rotten lie—everything they're saying!"

"Shut up, you"—Stallings jerked his head back, with a butcherous frown.

He knew that Rosenbaum was in all probability roughly conversant with the situation in the room and its previous phases, but the instinct to maintain his authority in the presence of the victims, and save his face, was too powerful. Rosenbaum called back to Alicia: "Keep quiet, Allie. Let me handle this." He spoke to Stallings again and his bloodless face was as courteously sneering, barely controlled, as the shade of voice which he used.

"So, my girl-friend's been cheating on me . . . raking in the coin. Well, well . . . it's a sad story, Frank. Honest, it's breaking my heart. Suppose we all have a good cry about it, out here in the hallway, and you can leave the girls safely in the room, Frank. They don't like to run down fire-escapes."

"It's oke with me, Joe. I've lost my handkerchief, but you can get yours ready right now. You're going to need it." Stallings had a smoothly nasty smile.

He pulled Conley's sleeve and the two men walked into the hallway, closing the door behind them. Alicia shuffled to the bed-couch, with Mona tagging behind her, and the girls dropped on their backs and stared upwards, writing their thoughts and feelings on the impartial ceiling. Unbalanced for a time, they were tempted to lump almost the entire masculine sex into one unscrupulous, hypocritical, offensively swaggering figure—an old hysteria in the endless trench-warfare between the sexes—but the resemblance in their reactions ended at this point.

A shade less self-honest than Mona, sexually, Alicia squeezed a blackly perverse enjoyment from her estimate of martyrdom—an estimate which became more intense to divert its own insecurities—and, prone on the couch now, she could have torn the faces, picked out the eyes, of the three men who had brazenly maltreated her during the present night. Mona, on the other hand, lost her indignation, inch by inch, and began to realize, dimly but deeply, that the three men were only trivial apparitions in an economic system which encouraged their latent cruelties and yet provided these cruelties with hundreds of specious and worldly excuses, aliases.

The rumble of voices ceased in the hallway and the sound of heavy steps descending the stairway could be heard. Joe Rosenbaum entered the room, a sneer still lingering in a weary aftermath on his face. He had paid Stallings fifty dollars and promised to deliver another hundred on the following night, and the transaction had been amusingly suave throughout, with the detectives insisting that the girls were guilty, but accepting the money from a professedly friendly desire to afford "his woman a chance to go straight this time." However, Rosenbaum told the girls that he had frightened the detectives into departing, and his lie did not spring from the effort to be consciously generous, or boasting, but was, on the contrary, simply a desire to avoid the useless argument and protestation, which would have ensued if he had revealed the truth.

After they had poured out their excited stories and exhausted the score of relieving explanations and anathemas, Mona and Alicia felt themselves slowly returning to a more securely civilized and almost incredulous condition. The recent, crude melodrama started to recede miles away from the room—a temporary respite made inevitable by all the torment of pride, accusation, in their youthful egotisms. Afterwards, the remembrance of this night would reappear, sharply, even darkly, but now they could feel only the desperate need for an artificial, quickly constructed, healing intactness of body and spirit. The version of ugliness, ruthless invasion, brought by the past hour, needed to be forgotten, for the time being, to avoid the sense of helpless risk. . . .

Nearly an hour later, Joe and Alicia were conversing alone in the front room and Mona was once more asleep in the alcove. Joe fondled Alicia's neck and shoulders with a curious, despairing, almost poetic restraint—poetic to his opposing reaction of disrespect—before he spoke again.

"Listen here, Alicia . . . why don't you let me keep you up, let me support you?"

"Well, I've got a bright idea I've cost you a little something tonight, in spite of what you said, dear. Isn't that enough?"

"That isn't even a good beginning."

"No? Well, I think it is. Besides, I *don't* want to be a kept woman."

"Why not?"

"Oh, Joe, I've seen them oodles of times on Riverside Drive, or in Central Park around Seventy-second, and they're *always* the same. They always have a little doggie, a chow or a poodle, and they always make up their faces too heavy, and they're worried sick because they're getting fatter every month . . . and they eat loads of candy and go to matinées, and half of them are cheating on the side, crazy over some gig' with a straight nose and sideburns."

Minus his coat and vest, Joe was lying on the bed-couch beside Alicia. The wall-lights had been turned off and a yellow-shaded, nickel-bodied lamp on the card-table gave the only illumination. Slivers and rectangles of dim light, interspersed with shadows, severed themselves to the accidental, impersonal poem, which, because of its familiarity, was usually disregarded by human eyes. Rosenbaum, fiddling with the fluffs and skeins of Alicia's black hair, was viciously opposed to his idea of the flippant, unseeing, self-protective essence in her words. He shifted his body so that he could look directly at her.

"You talk like the moral at the end of Fannie Hurst's *Back Street*. You make me sick."

"Oh, I do? Well, you can stop going with me and recover your health, my *dear*."

"Oh, why must you bristle up whenever I give you the least bit of criticism?"

"I don't mind the criticism, but I do mind the way you put it."

"So do I. I had a rotten night at the speak' and the flubdub I ran into here didn't make me any sweeter. But never mind that—let's get back to the subject."

"Yes, I know . . . *why* don't I snuggle down on my soft, little fanny and bleed you for all the money I can get. It's an odd thing, dear—some men simply aren't satisfied unless they're being played for everything they have."

"Oh, I know you aren't a gold-digger."

"But I *am*."

"Am I supposed to laugh?"

"No, it's true. I've known you for over three months now, and baby, it certainly has been a strain. You know, before I met you, dear, I went after everything I could . . . coats, shoes, chapeaux . . . it just depended on what line of business the gentlemen were in. And whenever I lost a job, I'd accept anything up to fifty dollars until I got on my feet again. I've never had any scruples about it because . . . oh . . . I don't know why. I suppose, because they were all out to *buy* a girl . . . oh, *very* indirectly . . . but out to buy her just the same, with the same, old soft-soaping to cover up their intentions."

"Oh, yes? How about the poor ones you met—the fellows with

five dollars to spend on a Saturday night?"

"Well, maybe it's been just my experience, Joe, but the less money they had the more interesting they were. I mean they were mostly dumb, sure, but I could always find a few exceptions among the poor ones and I never seemed to find any on the other side."

He tweaked her nose and was hostile and yet thoughtfully amused.

"Well, Miss Robin Hood, so you took money from the rich and slipped it to the poor, or . . . excuse me, maybe you spent it all on yourself."

"I did not. Why say, if I liked a fellow, I'd take him to a good show and a cabaret and I'd pay all the bills too."

"Well, well, didn't any of the gentlemen ever get red in the face about it?"

"Yes, of course, and the ones who did were the least sincere. That isn't real pride with a man—it's just a scratch on his vanity."

Her eyes, turned toward him, were uncertain, a little defiantly distressed, and arranging further defenses, as she fingered the black moustache over his thin, upper lip. Rosenbaum removed her hand, urgently, with the look of one who was playing with an old hive of sexual deceits, which he had never been able quite to understand.

"Did you ever, hmm . . . well, did you ever give yourself to any of those hopeful business men?"

"No, I never did, and I don't suppose you believe me either. You see, I was always flirting with the idea of being a kept woman, but then it was so darn' easy to get along *without* being one. When the fellow tried his damnedest for a week, or two, and saw he couldn't get me, why, he faded out of the picture, of course . . . but it wasn't much trouble to meet a new one, to take his place."

"For the same length of time?"

"Oh, some of the easiest ones would hang around for a month, or so, and try everything from flowers to rough stuff before they called it an evening. When it came to a pinch, I couldn't give in to them. I wanted to stand on my own feet, and work for my own living—it made me *feel* good, Joe—and I wanted to hoodwink all of those boobs just because ... oh, just because they thought they were so darn' sly and wise, and I got a kick out of taking them down a peg or two. And then again, I could use them to get just a few of the little luxuries I couldn't possibly buy on my own wages. I know it wasn't honest, Joe, but they weren't honest either. It was sort of like ... swindling the swindlers."

"Then when in hell did you ever give yourself to anyone? I know you've had some men before me."

"Certainly I have, but there wasn't a darn' thing mercenary about that. If it wasn't love, Joe, it was a mighty big, physical crush ... always ... and it was always just my luck to fall head over heels for someone with about two dollars and sixty cents in his pocket after he'd paid his room-rent!"

Rosenbaum's face had a wry detachment, like a separate host watching his body and hers.

"Well, your luck changed when it met me, didn't it? I'm not a rich man, you know that, but I *can* put my hands on thousands whenever I want to. What are you doing, kid—playing a *slow* game with me?"

She squirmed away from him, inch by inch, and she was hurt by the fact that he had failed to understand her, and discomfited by a sum-total of guilt, self-assigned, which she could neither analyze nor quite accept, and miserable because, after all of her words, she found herself tongue-tied now, at a time when she had the greatest need for words. Her silence increased his antagonism. He started to rise from the bed but she gripped his shoulder and restrained him.

"Will you believe me, Joe, if I'm really honest with you?"

"Don't ask me any questions—I'll make up my own mind about that."

She was angry now.

"All right then, you can do as you please. You're not a judge and I'm not on the witness-stand. I didn't want to fall in love with you just because you have money, but I couldn't help myself, and then when I saw I was in for it, I got more and more nervous. Just because I *have* been a gold-digger to so many men I was afraid I was going to be misjudged the *one* time I was innocent. That's why I've always gone to the other extreme with you. Every time you took a night off and we went to an expensive night-club I was trembling all over, and last week when I had to borrow ten dollars from you it took me hours before I could get up nerve enough to ask you . . . and what's more, if you don't believe me, Joe Rosenbaum, you can put on your coat and walk out of here right away. I don't care!"

She turned her back to him, burying her head in the pillow, and she was shaking with a revulsion in which she hated herself, anything resembling a man, and a glimpse of dollar bills forever in conflict with idyllic impulses and escapes, forever tempting and pensioning the more adulterated emotions in human hearts, beneath untold scores of duplicates, glib explanations.

Rosenbaum's instincts had been sharpened by years of travail and disappointment, and his wrestle with many different strata of life had equipped his skepticism without making it tyrannical, and he was at bottom a man with a considerable share of natural penetration. He knew that Alicia had managed to disrobe herself, in the furious, loudly disclaimed shrapnel battle between allegedly civilized men and women, and that she had shown a spontaneous disregard for the dangers of misunderstanding involved. While he was not humble now—humility being alien to his poisedly bitter nature—he felt a diffused stooping which was unusual for him. Grasping her chin and the top of her head, he forced her to look at him.

"Listen, Alicia."

"Well?"

"Let's cut out all this nonsense about believing and not believing. Of course I believe you—that's always an independent hunch, one way or the other. The trouble started when you said it was always your luck to fall in love with men without a cent in their pockets. I wasn't suspicious even then, but . . . well . . . you see, under all the hard-boiled stuff I've got to put on to keep the wolves away from me I'm just about as sensitive as a raw nerve, and it's easy for a woman to hurt me, if I really care for her—too damn' easy."

Only too anxious to dismiss the inarticulate mob of doubts and desperations unduly heightened by a dramatic night—dismiss them for a short time at least—Alicia thrust her head forward and kissed his hair and temples, and dug her fingers into his neck, with the playfully possessive desire to strangle, which is always a more real impulse of destruction than the woman imagines.

"You know, Joe, sometimes you're the most quarrelsome man I've ever met and then again you'll go for days and days without saying a single, nasty thing . . . and even when we're quarreling you never talk *very* much. Somehow, I feel as though you were leading me on, letting me talk myself into a hole."

The old, contorted smile captured his face.

"That's a relic of my experience in the Diplomatic Service, Alicia. If you want to succeed in that game—uh, profession, excuse me—you *must* hide your own intentions and make the other man show you his while he still thinks he's concealing them. The benevolent, respectable crooks, who rule all the nations, aren't particularly anxious to send frank emissaries to the other nations, my dear."

Hazily, Alicia perceived the wide, complex welter of lies and greeds, so shrouded and staunchly defended in every capitalistic country, and though she was far from being an active social-rebel, she had a healthy, fatalistic contempt for the entire affair.

"Oh, it's a dirty, lying mess . . . everything, Joe . . . but I don't feel able to break my little head against it. It takes all I can do to keep alive and keep some of the vicious paws away from me, like the ones I ran up against tonight."

Rosenbaum frowned, indifferently.

"For get about those bulls, honey. They won't bother you again. They're only a couple of cheap, bottom wheels in the sausage-mill, and as far as changing the good old U. S. A. is concerned, you'd have to send at least ten million polite robbers into exile, or kill them off, because you could do anything, and that won't happen for another hundred years . . . if it ever does. Norman Thomas will get a million votes in the coming election, but he's only a harmless, tea-party reformer. The capitalists themselves are even friendly toward him. They know he's just a nice, little safety-valve that keeps the machine from blowing up, that's all."

After the indecisive pause, Alicia said, smilingly: "But you're a capitalist too, aren't you, Joe?"

Rosenbaum sighed, and was self-troubled in the depths of his cynicism, but suddenly he broke into words, brittle, straight.

"Yes and no, Alicia. I'm a coward when it comes bucking the whole works without any reasonable help. I'm a damn' weakling, too. I like to drink good liquor and gamble and wear fine clothes. I'm not an intellectual and Christ knows I'm not exactly a fool either. I'd join the Reds tomorrow, if I could see any hope in it outside of a broken head and a term in jail. I haven't the least respect for the Communist leaders in America—the babies who write all the essays and spill all the gas but keep their own skins safe, while the followers go out on the street and get their poor heads clubbed. I'm a capitalist, sure, but I'll stick to the fringe of the underworld and I'll never be a respectable crook. You can lay a bet on that!"

To Alicia, at this point, Rosenbaum was almost a mental giant, deliciously voicing the stifled, hopeless little opinions in her tired head, though his reference to the underworld gave her a certain degree of conventional, femininely shivering removal.

"Oh, well... you're honest about it, Joe, and you're the first man *I've* known who ever was. That louse who tried to hold back my wages the other week is a worse crook than you'll ever be. Besides, I think laws were made mostly to give people a lot of safe ways to be dishonest."

Rosenbaum squeezed both of her cheeks against the sides of her nose and became flippant in order to return to a small room and a woman he desired.

"Let's cut out the heavy stuff, honey. Christ, but it sure is hot tonight. If you must stay in this lousy couple of rooms, why don't you let me buy you a nice, big, electric fan?"

Alicia smiled.

"Sure, go right ahead. See if I mind."

"Yes, you'll take something like that but you won't let me put you up in a decent place."

"Oh, Joe, let's not talk about it all the time. Please... and besides, I'm not going to leave Mona unless... well, unless she goes off to live with some man. That poor kid works pretty hard, I'll tell you, and ever since she ditched that kike doctor she was going with—

honest, Joe, I never could stand him . . . well, ever since then she's been down in the mouth and I know it, though she never lets on."

"Oh, I'm perfectly willing to rent a place for both of you."

"I know you are"—Alicia caressed his hair with a sulkily confused and yet compelled affection—"but Mona wouldn't stand for the idea. I know she wouldn't, and I don't blame her either. She doesn't mean very much to you, after all, and this three-together stuff just *never* works out. You know it doesn't."

"Oh, I suppose not." Joe's voice was a hopeless growl humorously subdued.

The dials of the little marble and brass-pillared, old-fashioned clock on the mantelpiece–property of the woman from whom Alicia had sub-leased the apartment—indicated a quarter after three. Outside, on the corners of Lexington Avenue and Thirty-eighth Street, the noises were intermittent against a silence which was tense and besieged, like that of a palpably rehearsed cemetery, wherein the occupants were neither actually reposing nor dead—the only silence which Manhattan Island knew. Taxicabs whirred, coughed, and honked, like lungs without souls. An ambulance rushed by with its wail and clattering bell, speeding to the endless city melodrama whose recounting was so naïve and far-fetched to snugly protected critics of this particular time. High-pitched voices, cursing, laughing, butchering the song-hits of the day, rose and fell occasionally from passing vehicles and pedestrians—men and women, boys and girls, inflated and coarsened by bootleg liquor too quickly consumed. A passing woman berated a man for his infidelity.

"You did, you know you did. You were trying to make her all night, and I broke my date with Charley just to see you, and . . ."

"Aw, I never gave her a tumble, not one tumble, not *one* . . . what's eating you anyway?"

Shrill and gruff voices spreading a drunken intimacy, a childish friction and jealousy utterly unaware of itself, and lost on the hard street immersed in its own shade-hidden concerns, and yet more symptomatic of night-life in New York City than a thousand corrupted stories and essays. And in the background the sounds sifted out to a wider crackle and murmur, like a million, insanely hasty dramas throwing off a million lies of religion, ethics and good will, in the two-faced mania of life in New York.

Rosenbaum had removed his street clothes and was wearing a pair of gray pajamas selected from the pile of intimate garments which he kept secreted in Alicia's wardrobe-stand. Alicia was still lying on the bed and waving one of the red, green and blue paper and rattan imitations known as Japanese fans in this country and given away as souvenirs by amusement parks, dance halls. Apart from diminishing the impact of heat, she moved the fan in a rhythm of deferred, sexual expectation, holding in check the more delightful, sap-laden warmth in her breast and loins.

After Rosenbaum had joined her, she kissed his ears and the niche between his chin and neck, and she had a whimful, incoherent sensation, which for seconds became immeasurably quiet against his skin and yet continually perpetuated itself. Sex is a poem when, removed from conscious and self-ugly connotations, it slips past the always partly unreal divisions of masculine and feminine—the old furore of sadisms and masochisms veiled, fearfully naked—and attains the great, relative freedom, the crazed oneness of mobility, in which a man and a woman no longer realize that they have different sexes, no longer realize anything except a deep carnality and intangibility too identical and impersonalized to find any need for mastery and submission. Utter sentimentalists are too self-pitying to gain this poem. Out-and-out animals, with little sensitivity, are too rendering and prostrate, by turns, for the poem in question. People, to any extent moralists in hypocrisy or actual fear, can never do more than hamper and bribe this tangible poem of flesh and spirit, and sincere ascetics can only achieve the unfleshly half of it. It is the comparative rara avis of sex and emotion—the rhythm of different bodies and spirits so strongly compelled toward each other that every trace of personal imposition must vanish. It is, in its last analysis, two opposite egos able to cancel every atom of deceit and arrogance in the liberating and equal touch of their flesh and its motives, something with which the gentlemen who write about Jews and Gentiles in love are utterly unacquainted.

Joe Rosenbaum was a Jew on one side of his family—the father's—but he had within him the best characteristics of his race: the feeling of alert isolation, the inability to be a self-deceiving thief, the high-keyed aversion to social injustice, the fatalistic patience in the face of material adversities. The worst, Semitic traits—the unctuous, cleverly persistent greeds, the religious clannishness as a sop to conscience, the inordinate passion for luxuries and fine-trappings, and the scramble of calculation and hysteria in social life—these traits were present in Rosenbaum, but they had been invaded by an Irish-Spanish mother and made more exotic, more inclined to question themselves.

Alicia, of Scottish and German strains, was a freak of nature, a throw-back to some Latin ancestor and a stifled mixture of boldness and shrinking, restraint and eroticism, curiosity and conventional refusal. Close together now, this man and woman could not entirely capture the rare poem hidden in sex and yet, for a time, they were beautiful to themselves within this little drab, obscure room. Twining legs, pressing breasts, in the visual music of escape, whose description is never obscene except to self-obscene cowards,

Alicia and Joe were always a bit apologetic, sometimes incensed at their inability to release themselves and sometimes almost abashedly happy, with Joe always in the ascendency and Alicia struggling vainly to remove the disparity. With lips and hands exploring Alicia's bosom, Joe was never quite certain of himself, and with her own mouth liquidly stamped on Joe's face and chest, Alicia could never quite desert the feeling of deliciously voluntary bondage.

The imminent street coughed and grumbled in a desultory slumber. The absurd clock on the mantel-piece magnified a piteous second of time. Joe and Alicia crept into the old, incalculable illusion of singing freedom—the old, wanton flight from earthly pain and boredom.

Chapter Two

I

EMIL SPERLING was selling newspapers at a dark-green stand tucked beside the railing of a subway entrance-exit on a Brooklyn street corner. Emil was young—twenty-three—with a plenitude of brown hair, the light shade of newly plowed earth with sand in it, and a large, steady-eyed face which bore the youthfully subdued marks of suffering and unusual poise. He had a tight mouth, which loosened only in moments of greatest abstraction, or happiness, and a firm, near-straight nose, and a chin which failed to protrude but was stronger than it seemed to be at a first gaze. Close to medium height, he was fairly sturdy above the waist and a hopeless cripple below. A victim of infantile paralysis in his boyhood, his legs were now supported by iron braces which terminated in a padded harness around his hips, and he walked in slow and painful jerks, though the pain, through the years, had become an enemy forced to be remorsefully friendly. He wore black corduroy trousers, a black cotton coat, and a tan shirt open at the throat.

The time was approaching five in the afternoon and the homeward-bound rushes, to and from Brooklyn, had not yet started. Women shoppers, itinerant business men and school pupils, climbed up the subway stairs, and idle visitors to Brooklyn, over-painted women trading on their bodies and well-dressed men, varying from office-owners to racketeers, descended the steps. New York City was nondescriptly yawning at one of its subway holes—the most concentrated and distinctive places for an examination of its breeds and cross-currents.

Perspiring from the heat and yet clinging to his coat, as though its presence made his crippled condition a shade less naked, Emil sold papers and counted change with a constant flutter of nimble fingers. He was averse to shouting headlines from the sensationally doctored news of the day, as other dealers did, but sometimes, when trade was slack, he compromised by intoning them in a conversational voice. A murdered woman's body had been found in the bushes of a public park—a woman obviously slain to prevent her from testifying at the impending trial of a laundry racketeer. A playboy mayor had been denied a re-nomination in the interest of "party harmony," i.e., unity among respected and popular thieves. A Socialist candidate for Governor had attacked the State administration—the old, harmless, earnest barrage of statistics, judicious arraignment.

Emil intoned these headlines with a wearily lethal smile, aware of the purposeless hates and deceptions behind the endless, printed yell of a confused herd and its trivially canny leaders. The customers multiplied. A stenographer, with an over-fat, pretty face under her skull-fitting, black straw, and an aroma of veiled, sexual deliberateness, bought the *Evening Journal*. A spectacled business man with a sagging, judicial face—moderately honest and liberal—purchased the *World-Telegram*. An old pharisee with a comfortable bank account reached for a copy of the *Evening Post*. A middle-aged woman, who might have been a conservative teacher, or social-worker, carried off the *Sun*. A girl with a vacant mouth and an air of intense, respectable, sexual longings, asked Emil for a left-over from a morning tabloid, the *Daily News*. A lad in the Boy Scout regalia of short, grayish-green trousers, knapsack and hiking shoes, inquired whether Emil still had a copy of another morning paper, the *Herald Tribune*.

Almost invariably, the general status of the customers could be determined by the particular paper which they purchased. Scarcely any of these customers noticed Emil beyond a glance and the small business of words, and a human interest, a grateful relaxation of tensely hurried egotism, was entirely absent—an attitude more prevalent in New York City than in any other American town, despite the farmer's elaborate professions of generosity and good will. These people looked upon Emil as a respected but decided inferior, and even the laborers, the factory girls, among them, were more inquisitive and yet essentially indifferent to his existence. Only the small politicians, hack drivers and loafers—who clung to a street corner and made it an informal stock exchange—noticed Emil, with kiddings and a rough tolerance, and they were doing little more than entertaining the tedious lulls in their lives.

Emil failed to return the compliments. These different faces, tarrying, disappearing, day after day, were unbroken lures to his imagination, and though most of their suggested qualities repulsed, or frightened, him, he frequently thought that he had discovered hints of clear ache and revolt in some of the rarer faces, and his eyes and ears were forever alert. He could instantly recognize hundreds of customers but he was never certain that he had finally classified, or denuded them, since he was naïve down to the core of his being and at the opposite extreme from a learned psychologist.

He was tired on this late August afternoon and frequently leaned against his stand, swabbing his forehead with a white cotton 'kerchief. The street had all of the unconscious majesty—the hard immunity of inanimate planes—and all of the animate, self-sordid specifications so peculiar to the visual side of New York. An office building behind him shot upward like an impressively petrified arm. The "L" train tracks and pillars, close to him, held the squatting straight line and angle which sentimentalists call ugliness, but which is, in reality, a sturdy integrity of form. But the contrast of human beings was everywhere.

A greasy street-hawker sold a futile stain remover to knots of credulous idiots who watched him rub out a blotch from his sleeve, without realizing that the blotch had been especially prepared to meet the ingredients of the bottled liquid. Two urchins struck each other in the face, wrangling over a crap game. A policeman rapped an old drunk across the legs. Two hip-squirming girls in light dresses exposing the lines of their bodies indignantly repulsed the hungry masculine stares. A taxi-driver tried to shoot past another cab and cursed the second driver for narrowly missing one of his fenders. A couple of button-eyed, leather-faced mobsters stood in the locked, rear doorway of the United Cigar Store on the corner and smiled as they arranged the details of an impending murder. The shoulders and arms of passers-by often collided, as each person refused to give the other the right of way, and the entire effect was infinitely unfriendly, childishly hurried, secretive in its frictions, and intensely carnal beneath all of the garments and proper avoidances. It was New York City, the yelling acme of incredible generosities and brutalities, never pausing to extricate their separate identities and forever squelching the few, isolated, original spirits caught within the major frauds of streets and buildings....

The hour swung past five o'clock, the shadows of buildings lengthened on the opposite side of the street and a burst of melodrama drew near to Emil's newsstand—that melodrama whose recounting was always so preposterous to the well-fed and sheltered critics of the day. A Communist rally had been staged in front of the Municipal Building in Borough Hall Park, two blocks away, to demand the creation of unemployment insurance and to protest against the eviction of tenants for non-payment of rent. The gathering—disorderly only in its shouted words—had been deliberately attacked by the police, and a riot had been precipitated. Some arrests were made on the scene, and the Communists had been dispersed into fleeing groups pursued down the streets by detectives and policemen.

One of these commotions rounded the corner a block away from Emil and came sweeping toward him. Hearing the noise and noticing that passers-by were dodging into stores and the subway entrance-exit, Emil detected the little avalanche but hesitated, not knowing its meaning, and fearing to desert his papers, lest they be pilfered or scattered. He had scarcely recovered from his surprise when the agitation surrounded him. Another squad of policemen had suddenly appeared from another block, and the Communists were trapped. In an instant Emil's corner became chaos. The scene, which had been so furtive and detached, broke into an open viciousness.

The Communists, ten in number, swung their fists, or cowered, with arms crossed over their heads, as the officers attacked them. There were eight Jews and two Negroes. The uniformed men used clubs; the detectives employed hands, feet and blackjacks. A middle-aged man in black alpaca, with his eyes bulges of fear and hatred beneath a bald crown, knocked a policeman backward and was in turn blackjacked to his knees and kicked at leisure. A Negro girl, with white teeth flashing from a thick, distorted mouth, was pushed to a sitting posture, after which two detectives drove their feet into her bare, dark-brown legs below her partly raised, dark-blue skirt. A Negro boy in his early twenties sobbed between a jumble of profanities, while he tried to evade the downward circles of the clubs. A Jewish youth, broad-nosed, sweaty and livid, was held by two detectives while a third one punched his face. Another Jew, diminutive and elderly, with yellow stumps of teeth still showing with a face shrewd and unruffled, dodged the clubs with uncanny agility and then darted across the street, pursued by a plainclothes man, while machines barely missed both of them. A Jewish woman, fat, screaming and powerful, struggled in the grip of a policeman, who fell to the sidewalk with her, punched her huge breasts and flayed her fully exposed, jelly-like legs.

The other Communists were wrestling with detectives on the subway steps. Emil hugged the side of his stand and watched the unequal fight with feelings of distress and uncertainty. The derisive cries of spectators, safely parked in window and doorway, and imprecations from the struggling civilians, told him that the victims were Communists, and he knew little of Communism in America except that it was reputed to be a relative handful of idiots and fakirs working for a social revolution and subsidized by funds from Moscow. His economic beliefs were still embryonic and tinged with the cynicism and indecision of a thoughtful youth. Observing the melee now, he saw only panting, maltreated, bleeding human beings, and every blow they received made his own body wince, since pain had been such a familiar and unwanted payment in his own life.

When a detective jerked the Negro girl to her feet and twisted her left arm behind her, to prevent her effort to escape, a blended cry and moan came from her, and the sound goaded Emil into action.

Aside from the semi-mythical, self-felicitating pose of chivalry, his heart was overwhelmed by the sight of a brutality which it could neither accept nor ignore, and protest became imperative to him. Hobbling forward, he pulled at one of the detective's coat-sleeves, and the man shifted a hand to the girl's left shoulder and turned, regarding Emil with a squinting, cold look that was scarcely cruel—the momentum of a machine, which could not check itself.

"Oh, stop hurting this girl—*please* . . ." Emil's voice was softly frenzied. "She isn't bothering you any and you're ten times stronger than she is. What's the matter with you? Why can't you just arrest her and leave her alone?'"

Short, with a great span to his shoulders, and a pock-marked, unmoving face under his brown fedora, Caslow, the detective, confused Emil with one of the Reds whom he had chased, and was, indeed, willing to mistake any intruder in the same way, not because he was over-stupid but because the overzealous sense of duty, the legalized blessing bestowed upon his muscles, was the only importance to which his buried frustrations could cling. Without answering, he punched one of Emil's eyes, and after Emil had fallen to the pavement, kicked him once in the side, before another victim distracted him. Swimming in a black cloud with lavender and yellow spirals and sparks, Emil lost track of events; and when he regained consciousness, he found himself herded against the iron railing just above the subway steps with nine Communists—the elderly Jew had escaped—guarded by a semi-circle of policemen and detectives. Other officers held back the mobs of spectators, over fifteen feet from each side of the prisoners, and the mobs were booing and catcalling, without rage, and seemingly in enjoyment of something which, to them, was a piffling, comical drama. Several of the Communists were bleeding from heads and faces, and two of them sat on the walk against the railing, groggy and seriously injured. The police telephone on the corner street-light pole had been rung, summoning a patrol-wagon and an ambulance. Now that the victims had been severely beaten, it was necessary to patch them up again, since no murder had been intended.

A few feet from the subway steps, a red-white-and-blue barber-pole revolved in a glass cylinder, topped by a white, wooden globe, and suggested a patriotic exhortation exulting in the rout of the insignificant enemies. Behind the windows of the Regal Barber Shop, Mona Farrideau had watched the agitation, as she stood in a line-up of two customers, with pinned cloths still hanging from their shoulders, and four barbers, including Carlo Tressina, the proprietor. The men had voiced a good-natured contempt for "the dirty Reds," and Mona had defended them, not because she was in any way a social rebel but because she was irritated by the complacency of the men in the shop, with their safe skins, and had a vague bluster of sympathy for underdogs of any kind. When Emil had been knocked down by the detective, Mona's empty dissension had changed to a sturdy, feminine revolt.

"Gee, look!—they've just knocked down that *poor*, crippled kid, the one who runs the paper-stand on our corner. The dirty brutes! What are they going after *him* for?"

"Aw, they made a mistake . . . didn't stop to notice. The poor slob couldn't leave his stand and he was bound to get mixed up in it, but they won't take him to the station, don't worry." Tressina, a slimly short man with a weak, protuberant face, was now far more perturbed than he cared to admit to himself.

He belonged to a class of New Yorkers who were indifferent to larger injustices but could be sentimentally aroused by smaller ones, such as a gangster attacking an old man or woman, an adult beating a child, a girl struck or "insulted" by a strange male. Mona had a much deeper rankling against brutish tactics, however, and when she saw Emil half-reclining on the walk, kicked by the detective, a roar filled every crevice of her breast.

"Gosh damn it all, look . . . they're kicking that poor kid out there! It's a dirty shame and I won't stand for it! I'm going out there and see if I can get the poor kid into the shop here!"

She was hastening toward the door when Carlo and another barber threw their arms around her waist and shoulders and struggled to restrain her.

"Don't be crazy, Mona! You go out there, you getta hit yourself! What the hell do the cops care? Whena those birds lose their heads, they paste anybody. Itsa not their fault. How're they going to know who's a Red ana who's not? They can't tell—they just hit everybody who'sa mixing in"—Carlo was actually concerned because he was awe-strickenly affectionate toward Mona and had always longed to possess her body.

"Sure, that's right. You can't help the kid now, Mona"—Jackie Traynor, another barber—a chunky youth with a buttery face—was relatively unmoved, aside from his desire to echo the boss, in the amusing manner of New York underlings.

In the midst of her compassionate blaze, Mona slowly began to realize that Traynor was squeezing her breasts and hips under the pretense of resisting her effort to reach the doorway. She squirmed away from his arms and pushed him against the wall.

"Say, you—if you want to touch me, don't be a sneak about it."

"Aw, I didn't mean anything."

The mote disappeared into Mona's dominant emotion.

"The hell you didn't—but never mind. I'm going out to help that kid!"

The two customers and the other barbers stood, like grownups turned into uneasy children, their eyes continually flitting from the outside drama to the equally compelling one in the shop. Tressina, still standing between Mona and the doorway, looked at Traynor with a pointed, Italian jealousy.

"So, you try monkey-business, heh?"

"Aw, I wasn't doing anything. She's crazy, she is."

"That's all right . . . never you mind. I talka with you afterwards. You can't foola me."

At this moment one of the customers—a fat, sad-faced laborer—spoke to Tressina.

"It's all over now, boss. See, they got 'em all jammed against the sub', waiting for the box to roll up."

Tressina shifted to the window, for a better view, and Mona opened the door and darted into the street. Tressina followed her, reluctantly, but a little bolder now that the main agitation had passed. Emil was standing wedged in between the Negro girl and the livid boy. His left eye was half-closed, darkly discolored and one of his sides pained him, where he had been kicked. Far from being bitter, he felt serene and even balmily detached, as though he had vindicated the existence of his crippled body and added his mite of objection against the stupid violence of life in New York City, which was always leaping at him from the print of the papers on his stand. In addition, though he still felt insignificant, to himself, it was a shade less passive than the insignificance of a news dealer forever taking coins from the hands of unmoved passers-by.

Mona spoke to Caslow, the detective.

"I want to talk to you."

"Yeah? What's on your mind?"

"You've got a crippled kid here—his name's Emil and he runs

the newsstand here on the corner, with his father. He isn't a Red and he wasn't doing anything, and there's no sense in arresting him."

"Sure, thatsa right—he ownsa the stand here. He's a good boy and worksa hard too, but... you know, officer, he doesn't wear a hat so you think he's the Red ana you go after him—" Tressina tried to be the apotheosis of politic chuckles, conservative salve.

Caslow turned to the string of prisoners.

"All right, Emil—step out and let's take a look at you."

Emil edged away from the others and confronted Caslow. His puny, bent legs, and the iron braces beginning just below the trousers-cuffs, together with the blackened eye, made Caslow a bit dully remorseful, now that the heat of battle had subsided and he had been informed of Emil's approved occupation.

"So, you run the stand here?"

"Yes, that's right."

Dimly, Caslow remembered that Emil had accosted him in some way.

"Well, what the hell did you say to me before I gave you the shiner?"

"You were kicking that Negro girl back there and I couldn't stand it—" Emil's voice was antagonistic without personal enmity.

"Oh, you couldn't, huh? That's too bad. Are you one of those Reds? Come on, spit it out."

"I'm not a Communist but I wouldn't kick a poor girl when she's down on the sidewalk. She wasn't attacking you and you ought to have arrested her without beating her up."

Something in this child-like, quiet-voiced opposition, free from anger, or words that might have been construed as an insult, puzzled Caslow's domineering impulse without in any way removing it.

"You've got a nerve, telling *me* what t' do. Those rats are out looking for trouble and they've got it coming to them."

"Well, this kid here wasn't looking for it, and you knocked him down and kicked him in the side. You're a brave fellow when you're going after kids and girls, aren't you?" Mona trembled at her words but clung to the writhing anger which had released them, partly against her will.

Caslow frowned at this feminine impertinence which libelled him and yet failed to issue from a man, who could be instantly punched. Tressina was frightened and tried to placate Caslow.

"Oh, she's, uh . . . just a little hysterical, officer. You knowa how the women are—they hate to see somebody getta beat up."

"Never mind that gab—" Caslow ignored Tressina and fastened his eyes on Mona.

"It's a good thing you're not a man, sister, 'r I'd haul off and slam you one! If you think *I'm* yellow, just trot some boy-friend of yours out and I'll show you different."

Mona was silent, checking her anger because she realized the futility of the argument. At this point, Jiggs Mehaffey, a fat man with a squashy, suet-colored face—one of the corner hangers-on and minor precinct leaders in the McCooey machine—walked up to Caslow with a confident familiarity and whispered words of moderation into the latter's ear. Caslow, obeying the secret master, altered his attitude, but with a manifest reluctance. In all calloused natures, a trifle of shame exists, and brutality is only the violent, indirect refusal of any person to peer into himself. Caslow waved a hand at Emil.

"All right, you—you get back to your stand and don't butt in after this . . . see?'"

He turned to Mona and Tressina.

"And you two birds button up your lips. You'll be getting into a jam, if you don't watch out."

The patrol-wagon and ambulance drove up with a clatter of gongs. Two of the prisoners had their heads bandaged by a police surgeon, after which they were all herded into the patrol. After the machine had rolled away, the crowds on the walks disbanded with a buzzing hesitation, as though they were loath to relinquish the safe superiority, the gleeful, law-abiding examination of beaten culprits, which had spiced their respective lacks and exhaustions. Mona and Tressina had returned to the barber shop and Emil was once more selling papers. The transition disappointed him and in his naïveté he thought that the arrested ones were happier than he was; they at least were united by a purpose and belief, pathetic and futile as it might be, while he was once more a secretly lone figure in a tantalizing rush of people. Even his bruises were unimpressive—a bystanderish accident.

Mona occasionally caught glimpses of him as she manicured an old man's hands and sat beside the window platform, where she was installed as a bait, which might be seen by potential male customers. Plying the orange-stick and polisher, with an expert series of memorized motions, which still allowed her thoughts to function, she found herself dwelling upon the crippled boy outside. His talk to the detective had been so direct and, well... not like a man and not like a woman either. She had no words for it. It was softly straight, like a boy with nothing on his conscience. It wasn't gooey, wasn't afraid, or, if it was afraid, the fear hadn't been impressed by itself. His face seemed to be intelligent, too—not so *very* handsome but... mm... unusual, simple and yet hard to rate. She had looked at him dozens of times in the past week without noticing him. That was a joke of life. God, how blind everyone was, herself included. What did a woman see in any strange man except a possible flirt, or a clothes-dummy, or an immediately obviously pleasing face, or just a poorly dressed zero mark glanced at by her preoccupations. Again and again, during the passing of every month, she might be brushing elbows with men, or women, who would prove to be tremendously interesting, if she spoke to them, and yet she ignored them, of course; and sped on to the certain and frequently boresome contacts of her life.

Yet it was not entirely her fault. She knew that the world was composed mostly of dull or tricky people, and she hated to take a chance, hated to be misunderstood, and again, during the few times when she did embolden herself—outside of cockeyed free-for-alls in speak-easies—the scholarly-looking gent usually turned out to be a grocery-clerk eager for three ryes and a quick embrace, and the handsome college-student thought that she was a plain hooker and immediately put his hands into action. Appearances and even the apparent looks on faces seemed to mean nothing, and it was even deeper than that.

Some power, mysterious to her, bossed the social lives of men and women in New York City and split them into families, clubs, gangs, frats, cliques and apartment-house circles, made them pass one another on the street, or sit in public places, with blank, stony faces. Displayed beside a window, as she manicured the nails of an old, marshmallowy realtor—his squarish face looked exactly like a pink marshmallow with human features cut into it—Mona discerned, mistily, the sneaking, economic system in which a minority kept a majority of human beings divided, distrustful and fractious, and still used this majority to serve material ends.

Her mind had been jogged into greater action by the swinging of clubs against skulls, which she had witnessed only an hour before. . . . Tressina had cornered Traynor in the rear of the shop, beside the closet where the linen was stored.

"Listen you—you keepa your hands off Mona, understand?"

"What was I doing?"

"You was feeling her plenty when we was trying to keep her away from the door."

"Well, Christ, where was I supposed to catch hold of her—around the neck? Maybe you wanted me to choke the girl."

"Don't trya to wriggle out of it. Ifa you hadn't gone too far, Mona wouldn't have said a word. I knowa *her*. Ifa you make the monkey-business again, you're fired, get me? Fired!"

"All right, if you want to make me the goat I suppose I'll have to stand for it, but I didn't do a damn' thing, I swear I didn't!"

After Traynor had walked back to his chair, he meditated on a possible revenge against Mona, but only idly, since he had a gullible widow on the string—a despairing, rather homely Jewess from Canarsie, to whom he was a blithely kidding masterpiece of indolence and youth, and the widow had a tidy little sum left by her husband. However, working scissors and clippers on the head of a customer, he relieved himself by throwing epithets at Mona. When *she* wanted to lean against a man, it was k.o., sure, but when the man did it to her, she exploded all over the shop. A-a-rr . . . women—two-faced down to the marrow of their bones!

The hour was six-thirty and the streets were wrapped in a frenzy of home-going people. Emil's father arrived at the stand—a middle-aged Swede with a leathery, raw-red face and chestnut remains of hair. Gustave worked at the stand from six-thirty in the evening to one A.M. and also relieved his son from seven to ten during the late morning rush hours. In addition, he allowed Emil to remain away entirely on Saturdays and Sundays and treated him with a vestige of gruff solicitude devoid of any actual understanding. Emil was an apparition offending the father's health and his prized common sense, and however strongly he tried to dismiss the apparition, a guilty quaver of distaste remained in all of Gustave's deliberately summoned affections. His other children, a boy and two girls, were sturdy and seemed to have all of the cautions and underhanded fixations typical of the normality worshipped by Gustave, without the nonsense, the bold deviations, which his prejudices detected in Emil's words and actions. The conversation between father and son was desultory now, occurring in brief lulls between the handling of papers and change.

"How did you get the black eye . . . dumb-head?"

"A detective gave it to me."

"A cop? What for?"

"Oh, they were chasing a bunch of Reds down the street and they cornered them around the stand, and the detective was kicking one of the girls, so I told him to leave her alone."

Frowning at his son, the father was divided between loyalty and recrimination.

"Damn it, why didn't you stick to your papers? What business was it of yours?" A pause. "But just the same that bull had a nerve, hitting a cripple like you'd like to find out his name and make a complaint!"

"Oh, stop that everlasting cripple-stuff. I can take care of myself."

"Yup, I see how well you do it. Can't you ever learn to be sensible?"

"I'll never learn to be a piece of wood, if that's what you mean."

The father grunted, too busy to reiterate a disapproval which his fool son never obeyed anyway. Then, after a pause, Gustave spoke again.

"It's always something. You trust that corner gang for papers and they don't pay up half the time—they flash a ten-dollar bill on you when they know you can't change it."

"Well, go after them yourself. I'm not interested."

This lack of business concern was devastating to the father, but he remained silent because Emil had once invested a hundred dollars in the stand—obtained through the sale of drawings to *Life* and *Judge*—and was now an official partner. After a long interval, Gustave spoke with a hopeless irritation.

"You're as much a business man as . . . well, as I'm a giraffe in the zoo!"

"Well, let's see—if your neck were a little longer . . ."

"Shut up!"

"Oh, don't be so *serious*."

"How can I help it with a person like you?"

Another silence intervened and then the father talked in a softer voice.

"Why don't you go home tonight and let Mother fix that eye of yours? You haven't been near the house this week."

"I'll drop in Sunday."

"What's the matter with you? Don't you like to be with your own folks?"

"Sure, sometimes . . . when I'm in the mood."

The father felt that these careless words were monstrous, but could not immediately clarify his objections. After another silence, Emil spoke.

"Don't tell Mother what happened today. She'll only worry her head off for nothing."

For a moment the father looked puzzled and jealous.

"Yes, I know—it's always your mother. *I* don' seem to count with you."

Emil smiled—the frank, remote smile, neither friendly nor relenting, which his father could never understand.

"I like you when you don't talk. I like Mother when she does. Let's drop it, Father—I'm going to quit work now. I'm a little tired."

He fished a pale-blue tie from a corner of the stand, knotted it loosely under the shirt-collar, gripped Gustave's shoulder for a moment, and then walked off, with his little, jerky steps. The father stood motionless, with a speechless resentment, doubt on his broad lips working up and down. As Emil painfully lowered himself down the subway steps, Mona, who happened to be descending behind him, caught sight of him and touched his arm.

"Let me help you—won't you?"

Emil halted and looked at her with the gentlest whiff of pride, quite humorous to itself.

"Thanks—baby can get down without falling."

They reached the first landing and stood for a short time facing each other.

"Say, it was nice of you to interfere when those policemen were going to arrest me. Why did you do it?"

Mona hesitated, not wishing to express a conventional pity and feeling deflated before the level inquiry.

"Oh, I don't know. I hate detectives. Most of them haven't an ounce of feeling in them."

"Well, I think it's silly to hate anyone—" Emil tried to be prodigiously judicious and then grinned in a confession of defeat. "But that is a bromide, I guess. It's even sillier to generalize about people's emotions."

Bumped by subwayites going in and out, Mona held her ground in a greater absorption.

"You know, it's funny—I never noticed you before."

"What's funny about it? The mailman drops into the Regal four times a day, and I'll bet you haven't noticed him either."

"Oh, no? Well, he's an old man with a nose like a . . . like a door-knob."

"You still don't know the least thing about him. Besides, there's nothing striking about me, except that I'm a cripple."

"Oh, cut out the artificial modesty, kid."

"Modesty, hell—I don't pretend to be of any importance. But suppose we get going; we're blocking the traffic—" Emil tried to inject a man-like swagger into his voice and succeeded only in an unintentional burlesque. As they walked through the nickel turnstiles and down the platform—still talking—Mona became desperately interested in the man beside her, though a protective hardness, forced upon her by the neurosis of a sordid city, prevented her from admitting the fullness of this interest. She had learned that people often strove their mightiest to impress a person, at a first meeting, with polished sentiments and a great assumption of candor, after which they gradually became more and carelessly disrobed, more violently emotional. But Emil's directness, his pathetic, helplessly bold naïveté, and his seeming lack of a defensive self-immersion, started to invade her unexpectant sophistication, which resisted the intrusion but could not quite dispel it. They were sitting on a wooden bench near the farthest corner of the platform, beside an over-rouged, pouting housewife in scarlet organdy down to her slipper-tops, and a young clerk in gray tweed, dreaming of the leisure and the plump girl for which he had paid so heavily during his bustling day.

Looking up at a station light, Mona was discontented, wanting to let herself go but lacking direction and competence.

"Do you do anything else besides selling papers?" Mona was unconsciously patronizing here.

Emil disliked her now, but he answered her because women in any way receptive had been so scarce in his life and he wanted so much the wistful novelty of examining this one.

"Yes, I'm guilty of black-and-whites and watercolors. The pen-and-inks are just comic strips—I've sold a few of them to the magazines. But how about you? Do you do anything except manicuring?"

Mona thought that she had detected a retaliatory sarcasm in his words, and after the first, simple irritation—the innately feminine aversion to being criticized—she peered coldly into herself. Well, what *had* she ever done, outside of different jobs to keep herself alive, or cling to the old bluff of feeling independent while wearing the beaver coat given to her by the latest boy-friend? After she had come to New York from her Massachusetts home-town, when she was nineteen—what then? First, a job as a filing clerk, and then the counter of a department store, and after that a renting office, a switch-board job, a theatre-usher's position . . . and now, for the past year, manicuring in different barber shops, because she could sit on her fanny and let her thoughts go where they pleased. Her silence made Emil believe that he might have offended her, and he had the impulse to be kind now—the softly spontaneous evasion of egotism.

"Oh, listen . . . I wasn't trying to act important. For all I know, my drawings are simply spoiling a lot of paper. If there's any difference between manicuring and selling papers, it's a very small one." Lost in self-deprecation, Mona's ego invented an ill-temper, to find its way back again.

"Oh, go ahead—stand on your ear, for all I care. I know just as much as you do, even if I don't think I'm going to be a wonderful *artist*, and furthermore, I don't even want to talk to you!"

Emil was inordinately sensitive to blows, not from an inferiority complex—the old, psychological rubber-stamp of explanation—but because the hermit within him had a pride which he treasured too much to submit it to the smallest hint of indifference from another person.

"All right then . . . good evening—" Emil rose from the bench and somehow, as he did, Mona felt that an element of newness, of crystallizing appeal, was quitting her life almost before she had touched it, because of her own petty retirement, disregard. She grasped his coat and he turned around and looked at her with a steady question, neither responsive nor pin-pricked. She had to force the words from her lips.

"I wish you'd forgive me. I'm a terrible creature. You don't know it but I am! Whenever I hate myself, I always turn around and take it out on the other person, but . . . won't you forgive me? . . . please."

Whenever another person became humble, Emil felt himself compelled to become humble in turn. He sat down and smiled, disarmingly.

"Sure, I'll forget about it. I'm a little the same way myself. When I'm not satisfied and I can't see any immediate way out of the trap . . . why I'd give a million dollars then, if I could bawl somebody out and feel big about it . . . but usually no one happens to be around."

"Don't you know many people?"

"Oh, yes, I know a few, but mostly men, you see. I was laid up in bed for a long time, and I'm only twenty-three. How old are you?"

The unmalicious question made Mona wince. Exactly twenty-six, she was morbidly certain that she could see the shadows of the thirties, with their growing, combated decays and the gradual difficulty of enticing young men, or holding older ones, and the feeling of intangible and impecunious insignificance, gayly, and sometimes vainly fought against on many a night.

"Never mind how old I am. I'm old enough to be wise without liking it."

"You're twenty-six."

"How did you know?"

"Oh, it's just a gift I have of guessing ages—the expressions on a person's face, hidden or otherwise, and the words he speaks and he doesn't speak, often jumbled together."

"Do you think I look younger than I am?"—this wistfully.

"Well, yes, a little, but not much."

"You're too truthful to live!" Her smile relieved the words of their sharpness.

"I'll start lying then—I'd like to live at least fifteen years more."

After a pause she said: "Good grief, I'll bet we've let half a dozen trains pass by! Let's get home some time; we can't sit here forever."

A string of cars came roaring into the station. They boarded one of them, providentially managing to find seats because most New Yorkers idiotically crowd into the middle and front coaches, and leave the two rear ones half, or entirely, empty. Talking to Emil during the lulls in noise beside each station, and sometimes trying to converse above the howl of the cars, Mona discovered that Emil lived in a small, Greenwich Village room, away from his Brooklyn family, and that his only friends—in a surface way—were people whom he had picked up in the tea rooms and on the park benches of that vicinity. Mona was appalled by such a loneliness and yet respectful toward its voluntary, uncomplaining, quietly inquisitive attitude—an isolation so different from her own existence between working hours, with all of her phone calls and dates, her escorts ranging from middle-aged business men to flashy, idle boys, and her occasional, semi-drunken splurges in speak-easies, night clubs.

It was a dope, a fast-moving, boldly laughing, or sullen, dope, to keep herself excited and make herself sexually sought-after and "choosey," and hold down the moments of smallness and self-boredom, arriving, sometimes, when they were least expected. Yes, she knew these things, during the periods when a blow between the eyes made thought compulsory—like the attempted frame-up of three weeks before—but it was an inevitable dope, nevertheless, and had its justifications. If a woman was without any unusual talent, any accomplishment which could make people sit up and take notice, then what was left for her except a mad running-about, a swelled-up trifling with men and liquor, or a wild love affair hugged in the face of the approaching disillusionment, until she finally married some man from an alleged love, or from a deceptively lingering, physical rapture? Then again, plain fear of neglect, in the face of her advancing years, or the weariness caused by a tedious job, could force her to settle down with the inevitable, familiarly uninspiring husband, and squalling, tyrannical kids.

But this boy, only three years younger than herself, was content to sit on a bench in Washington Square, or against the wall of a ludicrous, nutty Village joint, and watch for hours, or talk "art" with conceited pick-ups, partly, at least, because he couldn't foxtrot, swagger and run around like other men. Now that she came to think of it, being strong and healthy was not always a complete blessing—it inclined people to find such joy in the swing and tingle of their bodies that they rocked their minds to sleep and were more concerned with their clothes and their skins than with being independent, using their minds.

Lacking an engagement for the present Friday night, because the gentleman had been called out of town—his voice had sounded fairly convincing over the telephone—Mona, just as the train was pulling into the Chambers Street station, invited Emil to ride uptown and visit the apartment into which she and Alicia had recently moved. Faced by the probability of an empty night, outside of belated telephone invitations, never more than last refuges, her motives in asking Emil were partly selfish and ordinary, and yet that was not the entire story. Emil, even in this short period, had disturbed her curiosity, stirred her in a way half pleasant and yet frantically shrinking, and in addition, she wanted to investigate the departure of a man, who seemed to carry an appeal at the opposite extreme from sexuality. Emil demurred for a time, wondering whether the surprisingly quick "bid" was not an unmeant politeness, or a casual pity, but when Mona became insistent, he assented with words which concealed his uncertainty, eagerness. He had intended to sketch a bit and then go to a Village place known as "George's Rendezvous," where at best he would have sat upon a leather-padded wall-seat to the rear of the large establishment, and conversed with two, or three, condescending, amateur-adventurers, Village floaters—also relegated to the rear because they were shabbily dressed, or known to be "poor spenders." He had reached no definite opinions concerning Mona, partly because he was inclined by nature to be tentative and sparing, and again because she appeared to be flimsily ordinary, hard-tongued and humbly repentant in such an unpredictable succession that he could not decide which was the pretense and which the reality.

They changed to a local at Forty-second Street and left the subway at the Sixty-sixth Street station. As they were walking up Columbus Avenue beside the greasy, run-down, electrically pallid stores and glimpses of dimly dirty hallways, Mona was garrulous, unsettled, remembering that she had quarrelled with Alicia on the morning of this day and wondering what the latter's mood was now.

"We only moved into this apartment a week ago. The block we're on certainly isn't anything to brag about, but the dump we live in isn't nearly so bad on the inside."

"Where did you move from?"

"Well, we had a place on Lexington near Thirty-eighth, but the landlord was horribly rude. He requested us to *leave*. Imagine."

"What was the trouble—a noisy gin party?"

Mona's face clouded and her green eyes were blazing with hatred, with self-blame and its exemption, for a time.

"Oh, I'm not crazy about remembering it . . . You see, a rotten stool-pigeon and a couple of detectives tried to frame us on a charge of prostitution—just like that." (A sigh.) "It was so crude it would have made you vomit . . . and then afterwards, a pair of old maids and a fat, old sponge downstairs made a complaint to the landlord. They said we were bringing men to the flat and yelling about money. God, the imaginations of people when they want to be trouble-makers! It was really funny. As angry as we were, Alicia and I had to laugh our heads off about it."

Emil studied the sidewalk as he hobbled forward. Sometimes the totals of ill-will, misunderstanding and sharp-practice in New York staggered his naïveté and made him feel as though he were an unbelieving and yet almost convinced hermit staring out at a moon-disguised swamp close to his door. This night life in New York, with its bands and songs and laughters and back-slappings and fox-trots and radio squawks and gatherings all the way from respectable to naked—God, how many sores and graspings and jealousies and knife-swingings the whole array seemed to hide! And yet, after being overwhelmed, the naïveté continually reasserted itself. But the artists, the actual thinkers, the musing, untouched bystanders—they lived in New York and made a world of their own,

Emil thought. Even among the down-trodden, piteously strutting, marajuana-smoking frauds in the Village—barricaded in the few, remaining, cheap dwellings such as Plunsky's "stables," an Italian tenement-house on Cornelia Street, basements and attics on Jane Street, Patchin Place—he had discovered two or three boys and girls with tolerance and snarls friendly in their hearts, and a beginning bonfire in their heads, but they had conversed with him only a short time before other people snatched them away.

Mona and Emil walked down Sixty-eighth Street between Columbus Avenue and Central Park West. The contrast was insane. Dirty tailor shops, delicatessens and green-shaded speak-easies stood in basement areas back from the sidewalk, beside the iron balustrades and high front steps of old, chipped, brown-stone and painted brick houses. Signs blossomed in all the front windows of the three- and four-story huddles of lower, shady materialism—"Rooms For Rent"... "Light Housekeeping"... "Front Parlor Vacant"... "Stage-Dancing Specialists: Banjo and Guitar Taught In Ten Lessons"... Midwife signs in Spanish... "Astrology and Phrenology Expert"... and then, suddenly, two or three spic-and-span structures pressing against the suavely elite, twenty-story apartment-houses on the corner of Central Park West. It was Manhattan Island personified, where different worlds in the main trends of sex and commerce abruptly touched and inter-penetrated one another without the slightest sign of recognition.

Mona and Emil walked into the narrow, red-carpeted, plaster-walled hallway of an apartment building where children's squeals, family arguments, frying-pan smells and radio squalls drifted through the doors of the different flats. Emil was tired and permitted Mona to help him up the stairway to the second-floor apartment and the touch of her arms and hands, the occasional pressure of her legs, made him feel disrupted, swirlingly amused, and woebegone in a dispute where the emotions could scarcely be separated. Bits of anticipation rose solitary in his heart and were dismissed almost instantly. He regarded sex as a curiously worldly and yet ecstatic stranger forever close enough for him to feel its breath, as now, but forever marching away with a compassionate wave of the hand. Yet the loneliness in his heart sometimes became solid and could not be controlled, and he saw himself in the arms of a girl crippled like himself, or pressed against the body of a woman blind to his physical deformities because she had dissolved effortlessly into every cranny of his mind and heart. And at other times, after a day unusually filled with slights and insincere, syrupy pities from women, he would rest on his bed, groaning and pale with frustration and close to meditations on suicide until the latent, gentle elasticity within him effected a rescue and laughed at the preceding despair.

In his only full contact with sex up to date, he had picked up a prostitute on Broadway, paid her and passively submitted to her mechanical embraces and caught glimpses of her stolidly averted face—leaving her with a feeling of belittlement, dank disquietude, which had lingered for weeks. Sitting in the apartment now, Emil looked at Mona, as she moved around the room, with a wistfully checked, sensual intensity rare for him. Her hair, naturally golden-reddish, and the broad, high cheek-boned earthliness of her milky-skinned face, feminine without being over-plump, held a strength, a promise of restoration, which all of the unmaimed youth in his crippled body craved. Again, her body, stout but subtly and gradually balanced in its proportions—with a high, unapparently full bosom and long legs—gave him a feeling that was hardly carnality —a prodigious desire to sink upon it in unactively dreaming sleep, where movements would lose their coarseness and pressures would extend beyond mere violence and its gorged cessations.

Shifting uncomfortably in his chair, he sighed deeper than his flesh, and expelled these seemingly impossible hopes. Alicia was rattling dishes in the kitchenette to the left of the rear room and had not yet appeared. Mona, in her long, black velvet-chiffon touched with gray, seemed to be visibly and invisibly somber between the dictated artifice of smiles. Alicia slouched into the front room, drawing back the yellow portières which hung from black rings on a wooden pole. She was wearing an old, muddy-green pongee and black pumps, and her black hair, ending an inch below her shoulders, was a storm-cloud appropriately enclosing the present sullenness of her thin-nosed, brownly oval face.

When Mona introduced Emil, Alicia returned a curt hello and promptly ignored him, as she examined the dresses in a closet behind his chair. With his usual tissue-papery sensitiveness, Emil shrank into himself, barely keeping an outward composure, and started to hunt for a plausible excuse which might support his quick departure. Mona walked up to Emil's chair and frowned at Alicia over his head.

"Say, you . . . can't you be civil to a guest of mine?"

Alicia—shifting for an instant toward Mona—dug the tips of her forefingers into the corners of her mouth and pulled the corners back, simultaneously, which was her method of indicating a comically forced smile controlling the immediate utterance of an anger. Mona thumbed her nose in reply—the familiarities of women who felt that they knew each other too well to pay heed to etiquettes, but were not necessarily deeply derisive. Turning again in front of the portières, Alicia stared at Emil for the first time. Cuddled against the dark-blue upholstery of the arm-chair, with his light-brown hair disordered above a palely distressed face and his frail legs crossed, with the inevitable braces peeping out, Emil looked like a vagabondish child trying without much success to adjust himself to the adults in the room. Alicia found herself becoming more clement, despite the general anger of her mood. Emil was so different from the run of Mona's men that Alicia fell prey to a softly inquisitive surprise.

"I'm awf'lly sorry, Mr. . . . ."

"Sperling. Emil Sperling."

"Thank you. I'm really very sorry. I guess I'm not a fit person to mingle with anyone tonight."

"No, you haven't been for the last two days—" Mona frowned.

Alicia exploded.

"Can't you keep quiet, or must we have it out all over again?"

"Sure, I'll be quiet when *you* act like a human being."

"Listen, maybe you're anxious to air your dirty linen in front of Mr. Sperling, but I'm not."

Emil rose from the chair.

"I guess I'm in the way. I think I'll be going—I've got a sketch I wanted to finish tonight, and I didn't intend to stay long anyway."

Mona hastened to Emil and stroked one of his arms, just a trifle motherly in the midst of her tantrum.

"You stay right here . . . that's all there is to it. I'm not going to let Alicia chase you away."

Alicia, stepping to and fro before the portières, was troubled and more quietly angry.

"You're positively ridiculous, Mona. If I wanted him to leave I'd tell him—I'm not a very tactful person and you know I simply thought he'd be embarrassed to hear us shouting our private affairs all over the room."

Emil dropped back to the chair. His Christ-complex came to the front—not necessarily a desire to pacify people but to make them less strident, more direct, more desirous of reaching the bottom of their dissension and fighting it out straightly, free from the throng of little sarcasms, sneers, damns and hells, with which most people fortified their malice, from the bull-fighting novelist at one end to the slangy factory girl at the other. His reasons were nearly always two-fold—a physical shrinking from rancorous ill-wind, expressed with loud voices, or fists, and an aversion to the blind alleys, the minutely plotting circles, with which human beings seemed to perpetuate their endlessly veiled hatred, misunderstanding, evasion. He looked from Alicia to Mona now, back and forth, a diffident and relatively selfless smile playing with his tight mouth. The smile became bolder, more irresistible to itself.

"I don't want to be meddlesome but . . . can't I tell you something?" His eyes were fixed on Alicia.

Alicia liked the soft and yet straight concern of his voice.

"Certainly. You go right ahead and get it off your chest—" Alicia sat on the edge of a low, broad couch, touching the opposite wall of the room, and was a little more than casually attentive, her anger laid aside for the time.

Mona perched on a chair near the atrociously carved marble front and mantel of the fireplace, eyed Emil with an expectation which was peevish and yet intent. Entirely unconscious of the two girls staring at him—in any way of personal contrast—Emil gave words to one part of his little, deeply retired and nursed dream-world.

"Well, I'm only a kid, but I've knocked around . . . a little. Just because I'm a cripple I've had to watch from the side-lines, most of the time, and maybe I've noticed a few things I wouldn't have noticed otherwise. You're both sore at each other and you're bottling half of it up and taking the other half out in little sneers and digs, and, oh ... I don't know ... slaps pretending not to be slaps and acting very indignantly innocent about it. You're both heated and mixed up in it now, so you can't see how humorous it is to talk that way. Of course, I don't know what it's all about, but unless it's so *darn'* private that you couldn't *bear* to let me listen to it, well ... I think you'd feel a lot better if you thrashed it out in the open and got straight to the point. Don't you think so?"

From another man, the words would have sounded to Alicia like a lengthy and boresomely self-superior lecture, but she could almost feel—without seeing it—an aura of sincerity quivering around the large head of this boy in the chair. She smiled against her will.

"I think you're a rather nice fellow—no fooling."

"I don't exactly know what the word *nice* means, but ... it was nice of you to say it—" Emil's smile, much like that of a teasing child flirting with maturity and his words of the same quality, touched Alicia irresistibly and she rose, walked over to him, and ruffled his hair, for a second, entirely without conscious, sexual impulse and much as a person, older than herself, might have placed her fingers on an impersonally pleasing boy. Mona, on the other hand, with the beginning of a more emotionally intimate interest in Emil, resented the change in which she could no longer defend him against Alicia's lack of response. The resentment was not strong enough to be a definite jealousy but was more the squirming of an ego, which imagined that it had been outwitted by another woman. Her verbal tilts with Emil had all ended in uncomfortable silences on her part and her entire being dreaded this odd boy's mental superiority, the possibility of which she had been forced to consider. Jumping to her feet now, she circled around Emil, with a smile lending a nastily knowing twist to her lips.

"You certainly are a fool kid. If any woman soft-soaps you a little, you immediately forget all about her rudeness to you. Besides, I really wish you wouldn't talk like Jesus Christ. I'm quite sure you're not absolutely spotless yourself."

"Oh, *please*, Mona—don't be so small. We've both been jabbing each other like a couple of school kids, and I think he's perfectly right. . . . Let's have it out, once and for all—" Alicia was honestly disdainful, as she rose from the couch.

Mona accepted the challenge.

"All right . . . you were the one who talked about dirty linen and not me. You've been constantly cheating on Joe Rosenbaum for the past week, and I know it, but when you caught him kissing me last night, you raised a scene about it . . . after he'd gone. I simply don't get your attitude, Alicia."

"Oh, no? What's so mysterious? I found out he was visiting another girl behind my back, so I decided to get even with him, but that didn't concern you. He doesn't mean a thing to you and you were only fooling around with him because it tickled your vanity. You didn't care one rap whether you were hurting *me*, or not."

The two girls were zigzagging around one another, with the atomical intensities of emotion which are always so ludicrous to the sophisticated bystander.

"Well, if he *is* trying to juggle you and some other girl, then why do you keep on going with him? I knew that you were doing that to him, so I thought that you had cooled down about him and you were afraid to break the news to him, that's all. God knows, I'm not after him."

Halting, Alicia looked at Mona with a miserable, reluctant poisoning of pride.

"But, Mona ... I'm still mad about Joe. I wouldn't give one of his fingers for ten other fellows, and the funny part is, I know he's still crazy about me. It's all my fault—it always is. We had another big spat a week ago. It was the same, old thing: wouldn't I go and live with him in a swell apartment and let him support me. He went off in a tearing huff about two in the morning—that was the time he wouldn't speak to you when you were coming in, and then, well ... he started seeing that Stephens girl and when I heard about it, I got plain, fighting jealous and I rang up Tommy Burger. It doesn't take much to start things ... I guess."

Mona stepped to Alicia and cupped a hand over her shoulder.

"See here, kid ... if you've been turning his proposition down because you don't want to break up with me, well ... just forget about my end of it. I've lived alone before and it's not going to kill me, and besides, neither of us can go on working at some empty job *all* of our lives. You know how we're bound to wind up, whether it's the old marriage gag, or something else."

Alicia pressed a hand upon Mona's fingers before she spoke.

"I don't know anything of the kind. I'm going to keep on working, no matter what man I live with ... unless he's got *hundreds* of thousands and I'm foolish enough to marry him. I hate working as much as you do, but I'm not going to give any man the right to order me around and, oh, ... pin a c.o.d. tag on me just because he's keeping me up. Not me."

Mona sighed as she walked to the mirror above the fireplace mantel and eyed herself for a moment.

"Well, let's forget about it, old dear. When you get to be my age and you're still holding the bag, you'll probably change your mind."

"*Your* age. You talk as though twenty-six were a grandmother's funeral."

Alicia chuckled to ward off her own aimless blues, as she disappeared into the rear room. Emil had listened with emotions which he had not been immediately able to decipher—quick symptoms of fear, weariness and sympathy entering into one another in the unreceptive youth of his heart. The emotions cleared a bit toward the end. If loads of people, without any active degree of intellect to join their feelings, made the sex in their lives a squeezed-in drama and comedy of hidden orgies, jealousies, cautions, bargains, fights and contentments . . . it was not primarily their fault. The economic system, in which they were caught, invaded their sex too strongly with practical labors and exhaustions, with material hopes and bribes and with a general dishonesty, tacitly accepted and yet denied in every breath of their days. Such was the trend rather than the wording of his thoughts—his little, unequipped, indefatigable unions of thought and emotion—as he chatted with Mona now. She was petulant, uncentered.

"Baby . . . you think you're wise, don't you?"

"I wish I were."

"I don't think I'm going to like you."

"Then maybe I'd better be going-—" Emil stood up, but Mona, seated beside him, pushed him down with a vigor which drew a flitting expression of pain to his face. She was instantly contrite.

"Oh, I'm sorry. I didn't think of your *legs*."

"Never mind them—" A shade near to self-aversion possessed him.

"But really . . . why do you take every word so seriously? Can't you tell when a person means a thing?"

"Oh, I can in most things, but . . ."

"Well?"

"Do you actually want to know?"

"Of course I do."

He was silent for several seconds before he spoke again.

"You see, Mona . . . it's all right if I call you Mona?"

"Silly. Yes . . . of course."

"Well, I haven't been around with very many women, so far, and I'm not used to this . . . oh, I don't know . . . this social game men and women play with each other. You know . . . 'I like you, I don't like you, maybe I do and there's a chance for you . . .' all jumbled into one. It seems to be a rule never to show things plainly, just the way a person happens to feel any time, and . . . well . . . I've heard it all around me but I can't seem to get accustomed to it."

A subtle simplicity, a kinship to unworldliness in his words, drove into Mona and made all her fidgetings, weighings and unconsciously coquettish habits just a small shade unwittingly ashamed of themselves. She fondled the back of his nearest hand, spontaneously, despite her undecided mood. Sexually, he was producing the faint beginning of a conflict in her, in which her first indifference—conventional, taken for granted—examined itself and discovered fomentations disputedly near to a birth of tenderness. She glanced, alternately, from his feeble, abruptly slim legs to his large, delicately clipped face, and the contrast brought her tinctures of revulsion and appeal, whose surviving dominance could not be established.

"You know, you're an out-and-out child, but you've got a rather good mind. You're funny, you are. I've never met anyone like you before—I'll say that much."

"Do you object to the novelty?"

"Certainly not . . . goose. Anyway, come on, you strange infant. Alicia's calling us for supper."

The meal was a plain one of chops and a salad, with coffee and wafers finishing it. The three had little conversation at the table. Alicia was shrouded in her dilemma concerning Joe Rosenbaum and the other man, Tommy Burger, who attracted her, sensually, without biting into her heart. Emil was still a largely distant figure, to her, though sometimes, weary of her own inward grapples, she stared at him and wondered whether she could ever be impelled toward anyone akin to him—weakly distorted in a part of his body and non-assertive and . . . oh . . . high-minded and soft without being feminine—everything totally different from any man whom she had ever cared for. Yet this boy had a certain appeal, drawing first a woman's sparing condescension and then a sort of softly grudging interest. It was odd, new and leading to the light, an unwonted reflection that no woman could be entirely sure of the possibilities within her heart.

As Mona ate, she had a trouble almost surly in her breast and laughed off but sneaking back imperceptibly—a feeling which she could not define. Did this boy make her smaller and more purposeless to herself, and what right did he have to cause such an effect? What was in his words and manner that tempted her to see herself as a mass of . . . small gold-diggings, self-kiddings, affectations, ordinary dopes followed by a headache and boredom? The estimate wasn't a true one, but just one of her damn', emotional extremes! She had been as honest as she could have been among the rank and file of men—so many of them out to play a woman with every possible line—and it was in every woman's blood to be moderately coquettish, and life in New York City was, oh . . . a pain in the neck and an ache to "step out" and forget it. The devil with this Emil Sperling! Yet the dismissal was easy, too easy, without any trace of reassuring finality.

Afterwards, while Alicia was dressing behind the portières,

Mona turned on the inevitable radio—a small, dome-shaped one with a gauze-covered amplifier—and jazz tunes poured out—the smoky, blustering, jerky heart-beat of jazz, with its gluish adulterations in the flitting hits of the day. Emil had long been inured to the fact that he would never be able to dance, and the sound of jazz always came to him like a revelry from a distant world. Would he be the same person now, if he had grown up with an unimpaired body? Perhaps pain was over-rated in its supposed ability to develop people. He remembered the only Broadway party that he had ever attended—one to which he had been lugged by a young, newspaper reporter, who had known him in his early schoolboy days. At the party, he had met a much-admired, theatrical press agent, Nancy Revore—a middle-aged woman, who had been confined to a bed for years, as a cripple, and had only been cured and enabled to walk a few weeks before. Standing near him, the woman had released a flood of Winchell wise-cracks, strained gags and puns, cheerful bromides, butterscotch flatterings . . . poor, untouched thing. No, perhaps his own life might have been the same, crippled or whole, but . . . the temptation to take himself too seriously must be expelled!

Mona held a whispered conference with Alicia in the bathroom.

"When's Tommy coming?"

"He said he'd be here at half-past nine—" Alicia was far-off, disturbed, as she adjusted a light brassiere over her pale-brown, cup-shaped breasts.

"What's on the program, dear?"

"Oh, you know what. He'll trot me up to deeah Hahlem later on, but he'll have the old flask on his hip and he'll mix a highball, or so, and . . . and then he'll try something."

"Yes, I know . . . and what's Mees Aleecia going to do about it?"

"Oh, I'll probably keep him off this time. I don't know—I'm so sick and tired of everything."

"Well, anyway, you won't want *me* hanging around with my baby-kid."

"I'm not chasing you, Mona, but I have a hunch Tommy and the poor kid out there would get along like . . . like a kitten and a bull do."

"Sure, I know. I'll see if I can't go over to Emil's place. He lives down in the Village. Fakey, old Gr-reenwich Village."

A pause.

"Mona, you're not *falling* for him, are you?"

"No, of course not, but he gets in my hair . . . just a little."

"Mm hmm, I know all about that little stuff."

"Oh, stop it, Lish . . . he isn't a man. He's a baby, a poor, twisted-up baby. He's a nice baby though. Isn't it too bad he's *such* a cripple?"

"I'm not sure. After all, he can't foxtrot his *brains* out five nights a week, the way we do."

Feeling capricious, ill at ease and more self-bored than she had any intention of admitting to herself, Mona returned to the front room and suggested to Emil that she would like to see some of his drawings and water-colors. Eagerly he invited her to his room. His eyes were always instantly, profoundly affected by color and form and the present apartment made him shrink, with its faded yellow portières, its tan couch-cover dotted with strawberry rayon cushions, and its cream-chintz curtains sprinkled with hints of violets in a diagonal pattern. Again, he wanted to discover whether Mona would not blossom out in more private circumstances and show possible contradictions within the mechanics of a self-defense, which she had never quite deserted so far, in his opinion. He thought that one part of her was woefully transparent, with all of its little, slang feintings and disputatious bursts of pride, but the other part was much less explicable—the sudden probings, the quiet lessenings of vanity and the chastised smile which came to her face almost immediately after some spasm of ill-temper.

Alicia squeezed one of Emil's hands just before the "come again, won't you?" and "good-bye," and he laughed to himself under the pleasant sensation. Was she always so generous with her physical pressures, or did it mean more to her? These girls, he thought, practiced whims and pretenses to such an extent that they might be deceiving themselves half of the time.

Once on the street, he found that his legs had stiffened from too much sitting, and he entered a cab with Mona—a luxury which he allowed himself only occasionally, since most of the money from the newsstand went to the support of the Sperling family, and Emil allotted himself only fifteen dollars a week. His room was on the corner of Eighth and MacDougal Streets, in a three-story building of lemon-painted brick, which had once been an Italian hotel and dining place noted for its cuisine and sparkling Bohemianism during the heyday of the Village, but which had changed to a rooming-house now—abdicating in favor of the atrocious, Village slumming-heavens commended as "informal and pleasant" by the entertainment-guide of *The New Yorker*.

Outside of the rooms, the building was also occupied by a cleaning and pressing shop, a slightly Villagey cafeteria, and the fake, oriental tea-room of a Roumanian Jewess masquerading as a gypsy, who had amassed a modest fortune from similar frauds scattered through the Village during the previous twelve years. Unfortunately, however, the lady had neglected to install a minor jazz-band, a smoothly officious head-waiter, a curious boot-licking hauteur, and an air of catering to substantial, or flashy, people alone, thus preventing her inclusion among the other Village frauds recommended by the aforementioned sophisticated magazine.

But such a jest, so typical of New York City, was close at hand and yet remote from Mona and Emil, who were standing now in Emil's room and hiding their contrast of emotions. Mona glanced here and there, snickering to herself, at first, and then dimly appreciative almost against her will. Having lived in this room for almost a year, Emil had gradually induced the landlord to haul out the original furnishings and had supplanted them with purchases and decorations wrung from his savings. Knowing that form was only another name for the precise and myriad eccentricities of colors, he had arranged a scheme of indigo, vermilion, cerise and black. The walls had a black calcimine. The floor was shellacked in vermilion. The low couch had an indigo spread and a pair of huge pillows in cerise slips. An indigo chair with a sloping back, long arms, and vermilion cushions tacked on, stood beside the window—Emil had persuaded a carpenter, who was an acquaintance, to make it for a ridiculously small price. Plain bookshelves, lacquered vermilion, rested near the chair, and a low, indigo table, with one drawer and a highly narrow mirror, was placed in the corner between the window and the bed, with a black stool in front of it. The walls were bare save for a large photograph of a Picasso painting nailed a few feet above the couch. The wash-stand beside the door was concealed by cerise hangings.

Sitting in the single chair, which proved to be far more comfortable than it looked, Mona felt as though she were in another world, detected through a microscope below the towerings and the long, crisscrossed gulfs of Manhattan Island. Black walls, ow! . . . and a black ceiling.

"Doesn't it depress you?"

"Why should it? Black makes a fine background for cheerfulness. You know perfectly well you wouldn't notice the sun in a yellow room."

Emil, reclining on the couch, bore the wistful, airy grin which could transfigure his face, take the tightness from the mouth. Mona's wide lips beneath the broad nose—which had been straining to repress a laugh—became more serious.

"Say, you wouldn't. But, Emil . . . all these reds and cerises . . . ooh . . . it's like walking in the dark and then . . . and then getting punched in the eyes."

"Yes, but that's only the first time, Mona. There's such a difference between the impression you've got now and the one you'd have if you'd been living here morning and night."

Once more she disagreed with him and yet felt that her objections had been robbed of words—a new experience in the flip-tongued dominion which she had always established—to her own satisfaction, at least—in her contacts with men. She changed to one of the stools and crossed her legs belligerently.

"Say, I thought I had a pretty fair gift of gab before I hooked up with you this evening. I still think I'm right, but it seems you can twist words better than I can."

Emil sat straighter on the couch and eyed Mona with a sympathy which, somehow, was too unassertive to be offensively benign.

"Sure, it's all gab, Mona. Nobody's ever right, or wrong. You're not a fool and I'm not an idiot. We've got different minds . . . we've had different lives . . . we've been slaves to different feelings . . . and we're trying to understand each other . . . *trying* anyway."

Mona was disarmed, softly discountenanced and jerked an inch outside of her consciously known and habitual selves. What woman could remain irritated at a man who refused to parry, whose kiddings had the air of being partly at his own expense, and who placed his cards on the table, face upward, without any extra flourishes and with . . . oh . . . with a child-like wrestle against embarrassment? Maybe thousands of women would dislike such a man—women who liked their repartee to be hot and clever, and who wanted at least some trace of the old, masculine swagger and some intrusion, however indirect, of the old, polite, sexual boxing match . . . but this kid was getting under her blood. He was too damn' "good"—in the unboring sense of the word—to be true, but she hadn't located any flaws so far. Rising, she stepped to the couch, sat beside Emil, and pinched his cheeks and his chin.

"You're a funny, funny duck. Hurry up, say something good and dumb . . . fish for a little flattery . . . try to make me sympathize with you . . . try to make me think I'm a wonderful girl and I've got you up in the air. I *know* I've forgotten something. Why, of course . . . act very modest, oh, terribly modest, while you're telling me all about yourself and putting over what a great fellow you are. For God's sake, act like a *man*. I simply can't stand the strain any longer."

Her satirical flings amused him without causing him to pat himself on the back. If anything, he was too much at the other extreme—prone to an effacement and a diffidence, which would have amounted to a masochistic paralysis, if he had not been able to rely on the equally strong arrival of humorous indifference. He touched Mona for the first time now, holding one of her hands, pressing his knuckles against her nearest leg, with a gentle indecision.

"I'm quite capable of all the things you mentioned."

"Well, so now the cat's out. You've been *acting* to me."

"No."

"Then what *have* you been doing?"

Emil rose, hobbled back and forth in front of the couch with a serious concentration.

"I like to talk about myself, Mona, but I can never see much sense in deliberately explaining things. I think people have to understand each other . . . as much as they can . . . indirectly and naturally. All of this conscious helping really doesn't help much. When I said I was capable of the things you were kidding about, well . . . I didn't quite mean it. Certainly, I love to be praised, and modesty's a temptation to me . . . and I can be as mean as the next person, sometimes . . . but whatever it is I seem to come out with it, always. A man can hide his conceit . . . he can use modesty as a veil . . . he can hide his pettiness . . . but I never hide. I'm afraid I haven't mastered the art of, well . . . of social posing. Little tacts and dodges and sugars, and . . . oh, let's drop it, Mona."

Mona stared at Emil, in a battle of respect and resentment.

"Well, then, come out with this—were you slamming me, old dear, and covering it up?"

Emil became angry.

"I don't *slam* people, Mona. There are some things about you I don't like, but nobody appointed me to be the judge of them."

"What are they?"

"I'm not sure about them."

"Well, tell me what you think they are."

"All right . . . even down to talking it always seems to be a game with you . . . somebody trying to get the better of the other person. Of course, a book reviewer on *The New Yorker* would do it more smoothly, and she'd have a much bigger vocabulary . . . but it's always the same essence with most people. You seem to have other faults too . . . you get all tangled up in your own suspicions, and you laugh at something when you can't immediately understand it."

In spite of herself, Mona liked his anger and his direct attack, which interfered with her previous image of the gentle, charming and almost unmannish individual.

"So I'm just a blank in your opinion."

"You're nothing of the kind. Partly, you're what life's made you, just as I am. You can be beautifully frank and alert when you *want* to be . . . when you're tired of wriggling and hiding to yourself. But please, Mona, let's drop it. I don't know anything about you. It's only a first impression, that's all."

Ascending from the couch, Mona pressed her cheek against the side of his head, with a quiver which she could not translate into words or emotional certainty.

"Maybe you know too much about me . . . you fool kid. I hate to use my head—it makes me feel bad, and then I can't escape seeing all the rotten things in life, but . . . you're perfectly right. Let's cut it out for a while."

He showed her his water-colors and she saw nothing but lucid involutions and streaks of greens, browns, yellows and blues, bearing what was, to her, a far-fetched suggestion and distortion of buildings, trees, streets and people—not clear and friendly, like a photograph, but snatching a vestige of her puzzled interest, nevertheless. Afterwards, she rested on the couch, beside him, and they were silent for a long time. Her eyes continually reverted to his legs and his hips, one of which was higher than the other. If this boy were only strong and even fairly shapely in his body, what a beautiful beginning of a crush on him she'd have! And yet, even now, something about his firm-chinned, nice-nosed face and the deeply, softly unmoving, gray eyes . . . what was it? Something better than mere handsomeness—clearly pale and youthfully infinite—made her almost reluctantly responsive in a sexual way. It was a new desire to make his poor body happy in return for his thoughts and to lose herself in a stooping which might heal and lighten all of her dissatisfied vanities. She invaded the silence now.

"You haven't had many women, have you, Emil?"

"Many? I've had exactly one."

"Were you in love with her?"

His face clouded before it gave way to a tentative, disparaging smile.

"Christ, no. She was a whore I picked up on the street just because . . . well, because I was bursting over with a silly curiosity and self-pity, I suppose. She went through the whole thing with a piece of chewing-gum in her mouth . . . the poor, little fox . . . and then, of course, she tried to get some more money out of me, but I got away as quickly as I could, and . . . oh, rats, I'm not bidding for your sympathy. I'll manage to get along until I find some woman who can really fall for me."

The straight, uncomplaining melancholy in his attitude, and the palpably false bravado of his last words gave Mona a great, melting-out compulsion, and before she realized it she was kissing his mouth and cheeks, and drawing him against her side. She forgot his misshapen hips and legs, forgot everything except the youthful, unassuming hunger and the tinglingly spiced freshness of his face, joining his previous words to a concrete, living appeal. Even when she unfastened the braces on his legs, she was still blind to their conventions of deformity—since deformity, to be hideous or dispiriting, must exist equally in the onlooker and the assigned possessor—and the legs became only a pleasant helplessness, which it was her spontaneous privilege to console and improve.

Within Emil, the plainer delight—the almost incredulous death of a starvation—met with an almost equally intense dispute, since his nature was by no means heavily, or unimaginatively, sensual. He regretted that he was not in love with Mona—the love to which his tortured and often tottering idealisms had persistently clung, and one in which tangible and intangible meanings made the very sense of touch change to a silent but still living music. But his youth brushed the insufficiency aside, because this first experience of a woman impulsively bombarding him with her hands, her mouth, her breast, was too unexpectedly, exquisitely flattering to be resisted. His hands upon Mona's full breasts were actively and sheerly unreal to themselves, and his lips touched her face with the hesitancy of a child fearing that a closer contact might shatter the warm illusion of a joyous sleep. His sense of time disappeared, seemed to have been plaited into one, suspended strangeness, until the black walls of his room and the ticking of a black-cased alarm-clock near the bookshelves returned and struck him simultaneously.

He was still reclining on the couch, but Mona had risen and was sitting on a stool and eyeing herself in the narrow mirror above the dressing-table. A measureless revulsion possessed her now, in which, for a time, she could scarcely remember the past feelings she had had. As she watched him fasten the harness and braces to his legs and hips, he was not ugly to her, but pitiful and negligible in his body and utterly devoid of any physical attraction. The cleansing and diffusion of her spirit tightened to an ego which was once more calculable, conventionally earth-bound, and as she forced herself to analyze her recent emotions, she translated them into a foolish, motherly, unnatural kindness brought into being by the brave loneliness which Emil had expressed to her. This poor kid with his deep thoughts, his lovely, honest character, and his impossible body—she had given him false hopes now, or perhaps had made him believe that she was just an easy girl throwing herself into the arms of every man with a pleasing tongue and a sadness in his heart—a "first-night" girl ... self-beauty engulfed by the cheap averages of a city ... the rumble of hurt vanity, as ordinary and falsely prosaic as that of the streetcars below the window of this room.

Mounting to her feet hurriedly, she picked her gray straw hat and her black envelope-purse from a corner of the couch and looked down at Emil—a look that was sorrowfully self-reprimanding and nervously trying to be hard-boiled, in quick variations. Then, for no reason apparent to her, an outside remembrance intruded and she saw herself once more in the flat on Lexington Avenue, with the detective's arm around her bare waist and a secret, prone expectation waiting in her breast below the sacrificial desperateness which she had partly contrived. Good grief, if any woman were really honest with herself, she would have to admit the existence of times in her life—however rare they might be—when some dumb, vicious brute repulsed and yet overwhelmingly attracted her at one and the same moment. It was deeply a physical matter, sometimes hated, often denied, but forever returning to ambush most people. This kid on the couch was beautiful in his seeking way—stimulating and challenging—but something was missing within him, to her—some stupid, shamefacedly hugged, heaviness or blunt dominance ... and so perhaps she was doomed to go back and forth in her life, reaching vainly for some rare, sweet kid and then trotting off with a big-shouldered idiot under a black derby.

Unaware of the emotions within her, Emil brushed the straggling hair from his eyes, slid to the edge of the couch, and raised himself, painfully, looking at Mona all the while with a trusting, appreciative dependence. The strength of her desire for him, which he implicitly accepted now, gave him a delicious importance, physically, and made him ache to become fonder of her, not from gratitude but because he wanted to embrace himself, through her, in the beginning of a relatively selfless fusion so real to his sheltered ideals. Mona spoke to him in a rapid, jerky voice.

"I'm going now, Emil. I think I've stayed a little too long."

"Why, is anything wrong, Mona? Why are you so abrupt about it?"

"Oh, I don't know. This crazy room's getting on my nerves. I'm sorry, kid."

She walked to the door, turned, with her hand on the knob, and revealed a shifting mien—repentant, a little insincere to itself, and irritatedly returning to the hardness of the streets outside.

"I shouldn't have done what I did. I think I must have been out of my head."

A pause.

"It wasn't your fault. It was all because I started to sympathize with you, and then, before I knew it, I was kidding myself, too . . . but it can't happen again."

Another pause.

"I'm just . . . not in your class, that's all. I'm walking on the street most of the time and you're always in a bunch of fancy clouds, but . . . I like you, and we'll see each other again some time . . . maybe."

A shorter pause came, and then she said: "Well . . . bye-bye, kid . . . bye-bye." After which, she opened the door and departed.

Emil stared at the black door without moving his body and with an inner disruption which required several minutes before it could withdraw to identify reactions. Actual bitterness was impossible to him, and yet the contractions within him were, for the time, intimately related to such a quality. Inevitably, he misinterpreted the valid, purified sublimation which had caused Mona to yield to him and which had been knocked aside, afterwards, by the worldly blindness of another self within her and the temporarily implacable advice of past environments. So, she had given herself to him with a great assumption of pity, primarily to caress herself and to enjoy the great pose of a deliberate sacrifice unique in her life of dreamless twisting and deception. The voluntary beauty of desire, which he had assigned to her, had been, in reality, as practical as an ash-can standing in a hitherto unnoticed corner of her egotism. Women, women. Perhaps the mutton-faced, didactic German, whom he had met at "George's Rendezvous" only two nights before, had spoken words with a measure of wisdom beneath them. The German had contended, ponderously, that only four general classes of women existed—the housewife, the prostitute, the partly sterilized intellectual and the turbulent vagabond. If these arbitrary divisions were plausible in any way, Mona Farrideau was probably in the first class with an erratic dash of the second. But to the devil with all these rules and generalities. Only possible surprises and exceptions were interesting and formed any incentive for living. Some day his rotten luck would change; some day he would run into a woman actually walking apart from the fear-driven herds around her. He rose from the couch and tried, with all the youth in him, to bring himself back to intrenchment and reborn hope....

Striding down Eighth Street, Mona settled into her street expression—the sharp-eyed, distrustful, self-preening look, or straight-ahead stare, with which so many New Yorkers pass one another. She thought it necessary to walk with a moderate swiftness, since a slower pace, a loitering before shop windows, was apt to encourage the usual male searchers, who arrived at the conclusion that the woman was without a fixed destination and possibly waiting to be approached. The time was nearing midnight, but Eighth Street was still ablaze with signs and irregularly thick with pedestrians, and people leaving automobiles, most of them on their way to and from the inevitable parties or places of public entertainment. Shrieks and loud words from groups of men and women—more frankly demonstrative under the drip of alcohol and reaching for the old, half-bound animal relaxation—ascended and died endlessly on the waves of summer air.

The night was unwontedly cool, close to the end of August, and above the visual, eastern end of the street a new round moon stood in the clear sky, seemingly directly over the flat, uneven tops of Astor Place, and stared down with the bland yellow indifference of another world. The moon seemed to be a shining hole, through which all the baffled imagination of the earth could escape without remembering the transition. The night life of New York City was barely reviving from its relative summer apathies. A few last stragglers departed from the squeezed-in lobby of a movie house fronted by triangles of black and white—a place which had once opened its doors with all the promise and fanfare of an art theatre dedicated to unusual films and which had subsequently receded to the display of second-run, commercial pictures, in the inevitable turn-about so typical of New York. A cabaret was located a few numbers below the theatre, under the name of "The Village Cabin," with a front of bark and imitation logs, and a young, hard-faced doorman parading on the sidewalk, and dressed in boots, overalls, gray-and-white checked shirt and a high-crowned straw hat. The cabaret was a Broadway encroachment with manufactured noise and slyly smiling hostesses, and it was patronized and admired by those who insisted that Greenwich Village was no longer in existence as a separate unit—an insistence purely and simply an image of their hopes.

Mona lingered before the entrance of the cabaret because she knew one of the entertainers and was idly tempted to pay him a visit and drink herself back to normality. The doorman sidled up to her with a polite but keenly appraising smirk.

"Looking for somebody, Miss?"

Turning her eyes to the man, Mona suddenly realized that she was still out of tune with small words and merriments—still disturbed, inwardly withdrawn.

"I'm not looking for you—" She gave him a frown and walked away, and he promptly called after her: "Take your chin down, baby," a remark which she ignored.

She stood on a corner of Eighth Street and Sixth Avenue—not caring to return to the apartment, where Alicia might still be holding forth with Burger. As she wondered what her next move should be—sorting 'phone numbers in her mind and rejecting them because of the lateness of the hour—a tall man in a gray suit collided with one of her shoulders, in his veering to avoid another person, and halted to apologize. She recognized him as Stanley Bingham, a Wall Street clerk in his early thirties, whom she had met at a party several weeks before and who had escorted her to a theatre and a night club on two occasions. She smiled mechanically and they began a conversation. She liked Bingham, definitely but without tremors, because he had a fairly humorous poise, for the most part, and was moderately agreeable to her in a sexual way and willing to play a waiting game without becoming "too fresh"—a man included among at least half a dozen others under the same general heading. They stood on the corner and verbally sparred with each other, and she was glad to say any empty thing that might ease the strain within her.

"What are you doing down in the Village, Stan?"

"Oh, I had to lug a bunch of papers to one of my bosses."

"Hmm, 1 see. What was the matter, Stan—did she send you

home early?"

Bingham grinned.

"She's got a hang-over and a bad temper, if you mean the one I saw earlier this evening. But how about you, cutie? Did the gentleman pass out, or was he sore about something?"

The last remark supported Mona's remembrance of Emil, with an extra vividness, and she became irritated at the other man's unconscious trespass.

"Never mind about that, and don't try to be so funny."

Bingham eyed her with a puzzled attempt to understand.

"I didn't mean to butt in on anything private, Mona. You know I'm not that kind."

Realizing his lack of blame, and vexed with herself, she smiled again.

"Of course you didn't. I'm just in a bad mood tonight, Stan."

"Well, to tell you the truth, I'm a little down in the mouth myself. Maybe we ought to call on a good doctor I know."

"Oh, yes? What does he specialize in?"

"Well, his side-cars are fairly good, but the rickeys he serves just can't be equalled, and if you've got a weakness for real Black and White—"

"He isn't a doctor. He's the fellow who gets a commission from the doctors because he makes a lot of patients for them."

"Have it your way, sweetness, but . . . what do you say? Suppose we hop a cab and drop in for a round or so?"

"Have I been there before, Stan?"

"Not to my sober knowledge. It's a speak' on Forty-eighth near Seventh, and it's a swell one too."

Mona hesitated. The burning flood could destroy her sense of disgust, of indistinct discrimination, and blot out the dodging remembrance of Emil's dizzily hurt face, just before she closed the door behind her, but she knew, also, that the alarm-clock would awaken her at nine in the morning and that she might rise with her present mood all the more morosely intensified.

"Gee, I don't know, Stan. I want to and I don't want to. If I get cock-eyed tonight, I know exactly what will happen—I'll start to tear the walls apart."

"Well, what of it? They won't be black walls anyway."

"Ow . . . for Pete's sake, Stanley, are you psychic?"

"What's the idea of that question?"

"Oh, never mind. Come on, let's go. I'll feel just as rotten whether I drink or not, so it doesn't matter—" The picture of the room, from which she had fled so recently, had been changed to a repellent exaggeration and she wanted to drive it away, no matter what the cost might be. It was the childish effort to banish a feeling of guilt—which persisted in ignoring itself and yet would not quite die—in the manner of an actual ten-year-old spitefully destroying the emptied pie-plate which had caused him to be punished.

After they were seated in the cab and shooting uptown, Stanley looked at Mona with a truce between pessimism and anticipation, not quite as composed as he sought to make it. He thought that a man could never really understand girls like Mona, who drank heavily on occasion and seemed to have few inhibitions, and yet made a man respect them more than he respected the rampantly decent ones or the ones always flirting under a cloak of virtue, professed or real. He remembered the final minutes of his previous night with Mona when, standing in the hallway with him, she had said: "You can put your hands on me, if you want to. I'd get a little kick out of it, Stan, if you did . . . but I'm not going to ask you into the flat because I don't want you enough. If I ever do want you . . .

believe me . . . I'll pull you up the stairs myself. You won't need to make any desperate plays for *me*."

Wasn't it the eighth miracle to meet *any* girl who made her intentions and her shifting moods clear, right from the gong? Yet, in another way he hated Mona. In usurping the privilege of masculine candor, she placed him in a position not precisely effeminate, but one in which he was robbed of initiative, triumphant maneuvering—an interpretation searing to his vanity. Thinking to himself in the cab, he decided that he would emulate this curt independence. If she resisted a sensual invitation, he would escort her to her door-step and then say, immediately: "All right, babe. I'm out of the picture from now on and it's your next move. If you make up your mind you want to get serious with me, you can ring me up, or drop me a line. Bye-bye . . . babe," after which he would abruptly depart. After all, what chance did a man have with women of any kind unless he used their own tactics? The same chance that a man in the trenches had, waiting for a war-tank to roll over him!

Take the girl he had left earlier in the night. First she produced a pint of rye from her own kitchenette. Then she swallowed the drinks straight, without changing a muscle in her face. Then she joked about a book entitled *Is Sex Necessary?*, which was lying on the table. Then she gossiped broadly about the sexual diversions among her girl-friends. Then she allowed him to kiss her several times, and *then* she *cried*—big tears rolling down her face—when he began to touch her body freely.

"Please, Stanley . . . please don't make it ugly, just because I'm a little drunk. I don't want it to happen that way."

It was certainly a fact—a man could count himself to sleep trying to add up all of their dodges and poses, Bingham thought.

Bingham was thirty-one, with naturally oily black hair and

a fair-skinned face, steep-nosed, square-jawed. His face was an adulteration of earth, no longer direct, and struggling between the fetishes of ethics and covetous disregard. He had been a second-string tackle during his college days, studying barely enough to squirm through his classes. He possessed a narrow version of intelligence, efficient within its limits, smoothly practical, and making an effort to be "reasonably liberal"—one of the fractional variations in a New York City norm, midway between Boss Curry and H. L. Mencken.

"Stan, what do you think of all this higher-art stuff—I mean the stuff that doesn't look like anything a person can see with his own eyes?"

"Well, I'm up a tree. A great deal of it seems crazy, or plain fakey, to me, but I don't want to be in too much of a hurry about laughing. After all, I read a book about Whistler some time ago—you know, Whistler, the famous painter—and they were all handing him the Bronx when he was alive. You can't always be sure, Mona."

"No, I suppose not," Mona sighed.

She had wanted Bingham to make a derisive answer which might have aided her in quelling the shred of resentful uncertainty in her head.

"D'you know, Stan . . . life's entirely too deep for *me* . . . sometimes. Every time I begin to think, I get in lower and lower without finding anything out, and then I've simply *got* to come up for air."

"Well, sure . . . but what's the sense of being pessimistic about it? I can see lots of lousy things, lots of things hard to understand, sure . . . but then again, there are plenty of good, clear, attractive things, too, if a person keeps on hunting for them."

The words brought nothing to Mona except a vaguely hopeful agreement consciously manufactured to oppose her underlying mood. Peculiar, the difference between men—Stanley and Emil. Oh, the devil with that kid! The man beside her was more of a sturdy jumble, like herself—capable of being mean and small sometimes, but real and reassuring—in spite of the fact that his main appeal was only a possible sexual pleasure. Only? Well, take the sex away from everyone on earth and what would happen? Baby, there'd be two thousand suicides a day in New York City alone, and seven-eighths of the cabarets and dancing places would be closed inside of a month, and as for the theatres! . . .

After leaving the cab, Stanley and Mona walked down a narrow, blue-carpeted hallway, which had the air and smell of a baleful apathy counteracted by a wisp of feminine perfume. Stanley pressed a buzzer beside a broad oak- and iron-stripped door. A panel in the door slipped back and he offered the inevitable card with a dash of pen-and-ink writing, since the place was a large one and the door-tenders on the night-shifts were frequently changed. The door opened and they sallied into the precincts. The interior would have given an old-time saloon apoplexy. The long bar was an aquarium of thick, almost unbreakable glass, filled with fishes, eels, conch shells and sea-weed. The murals above and behind the bar, framed by thickly jutting oak, depicted scenes such as: a child peering below the shutters of a by-gone family-entrance, a tramp stooping to pick up a coin while a cop booted him in the rear, a nude girl thumbing her nose at a lurching pair of males in full dress and other, overworked street-level versions of humor.

The seats before the bar were dark-green barrels with bronze rungs. The walls were made of inlaid-wood patterns and dotted with copies of old-masters in golden frames. The square tables had white cloths and glass vases of freshly cut flowers and the wall-benches showed a deeply padded, dull red leather. In the midst of this pretentious hodge-podge, the men and women, served by waiters in tuxedos, were equally disorganized. The convivial guests steadily but irregularly directed glances and stares of condescension, hostility and unreal indifference at one another. The contrasting merriments gave the impression that they were neither happy nor haphazard, but routined or frenziedly incomplete. A friction lurked between the laughters, flaring up sometimes, and forever on the verge of proclaiming itself. A spirit of caustic snobbishness, based on money and clothes, collided uneasily with its own democratic masquerades, let-downs, and the result was a far-fetched hilarity always suspicious of itself, except in those cases where the participants were so drunk that they became unconscious of their words and actions. It was a condition peculiar to the public drinking of New York City, but qualified in the lowest speak-easies on Tenth Avenue and the East Side, where liquor sometimes made the under-dogs conscious of a buried, surly, proletarian resentment....

Mona and Stanley sat on a wall-bench close to one of the corners. After they had downed their second rye highball, Mona became more silent and Stanley more talkative, since his imbibing on this night had commenced before their street-corner meeting. He began to boast of his business successes.

"Baby, I sure made a nice little clean-up last week. I overheard a talk on one of my bosses' private phones, see . . . and then I spread a few bucks on Consolidated Gas. The damn' stock went up two points and I made five hundred dollars on it, and believe me, if a man can take even that much out of the bear-cave nowadays, he's a miracle-worker."

"Well, you ought to be sitting pretty in that case—" Mona's attempted interest was scarcely a shade above a listless voice.

"*Ought* to is right. After I paid some of my bills, I'd hate to tell you what I had left. But that doesn't worry me any. When this damn' depression stops I'll be riding high again. I'm working on the inside now and I'm just waiting until Mr. Bull wakes up and sharpens his horns. Baby, just watch me, then."

"Stanley, call that waiter, will you?"

Mona's lack of interest was palpable now, and Bingham frowned as he ordered the third round. Wasn't that exactly like a certain breed of girls in New York? he thought. They were only too willing to share the benefits of a man's money but they didn't care one damn about where it came from—never showed the least concern over the brain-twists required to bring it to his pockets. Mona was the last girl on earth he would ever marry . . . or was she? The other side gave him a pain in the neck, too. Women buyers, office-managers, bookkeepers, secretaries, eager to talk about the ins and outs of the business world and often knowing them better than men did—what peculiarity did a poor guy have left for himself? His pants and his shirts, that was about all. . . . Stanley was muddled, caught between flimsy, squeamish prejudices strengthened by liquor.

"Money doesn't worry *you* much, babe."

"Oh, it doesn't? Then when I dig into nails every day for twenty a week, I must be dreaming."

"That's not the point. A man'll spend that much on a girl in one night, but *she* takes it for granted."

"If I remember right, I didn't ask you to bring me here—" Mona was coldly angry now.

Stanley, not even sure of his own position, berated his quick tongue and made haste to retrieve his sexual prospects.

"Well, what are you getting so sore about?" He tried to speak cajolingly. "I'm not a cheap sport, Mona . . . that's not it . . . but every time I talk about some deal I've put through, you act like you had cotton in your ears."

"Maybe I have. I warned you I was in a bad mood tonight. I like you, but I'm not wrapped up in everything you say."

Stanley forced himself to be mollified. The liquor in his veins advised him to be careless, to take them as they came. The rye gave him a feeling of sexual invincibility. Seeping into his eyes, the rye changed Mona to a fleshly paradise too sweet to be offended. His hands couldn't leave her arms, the back of her neck.

"You know, you're a lovely thing, Mona . . . a lovely kid. You've got the nicest eyes and face I've ever seen."

Mona was still silent, with her eyes turned away from him.

"What's the matter, sweetness—lost your tongue?"

Mona looked at him with a coolly sullen appraisal. Good-looking animal, wasn't he? When he touched her, one part of her wanted to purr, to respond comfortably, but the other part was unimpressed.

"You say all those things when you're sober, Stan, and I'll pay more attention."

"Get out, I'm sober as a judge."

"Oh, Stan, you can't be as drunk as all that."

"Stop kidding, Mona. The trouble with you is you're a couple of miles behind me. You need another drink."

He called the waiter and continued to lavish compliments until the drinks arrived. He was half sincere and half alcoholic because, beneath the surface judgments necessary to his vanity, he had always respected Mona as a largely unknown quantity—an array of candors, inattentions and then, suddenly, a delicious response, emerging when it was lease expected and yet bearing none of the earmarks of a coquette.

The fourth highball burned its way into Mona's blood and wrought an immense change. Previously she had been tentative and absent-minded—staring at the formless presence of Emil, in the distance, without naming it, and then, under the stir of memory, awakening to half-hearted sneers at the former abstraction. At such intervals, she had returned to Stanley with an almost commended gratitude, drinking a little more urgently to increase his appeal to her. Now, for no reason apparent to her tired mind, she became enormously angry—angry at herself, at the world, at Stanley, and at the people surrounding her. She tried to circumvent this feeling, to swerve into the sturdy courtship of the man beside her, and she allowed him to kiss her mouth, stroke her covered legs under the table, but when she had emptied the fifth glass, the anger slipped back with double force, became clearer to itself.

Why was Bingham . . . half speaking, tactful . . . so God-damn' patient in spite of his drinks . . . when she knew and he knew exactly what he wanted. That was why he drank, why they all drank—to get bolder, forget that they were supposed to have at least some degree of good breeding. Even the out-and-out roughnecks, hookers, needed a good jolt of rye to make them fearlessly frank, unless they were unusually angry or desperate. Look at these people at the tables, at the bar—and what were they trying to do? They were literally flooding themselves with booze to *make* themselves act sincerely, just like her own damn' self . . . or to make their tricks more cunning and determined. Where in hell was a human being who talked and acted when he was cock-eyed almost exactly as he did when he was sober—who drank because he wanted to laugh at all the ugliness in the world, or because . . . he wanted to make it important enough to insult it, fight against it?

Mona hid behind her silent frown, which Stanley, beginning to be just a trifle blurred in his mind, interpreted as an amazingly quiet effort to control her desire for him. Hurray for a girl who didn't spread herself over the entire place when she was becoming blotto—didn't start to sing or blabber or laugh like an "L" train or try to pick a fight! 'Ray for Mona and himself—just a pair of wise ones, no doubt about that, and could they hold their drinks? Could they! . . .

Two other couples were seated on both sides of Mona and Stanley, and a party of four occupied the table directly in front of them. The pair to the left laughed immoderately—a stout man in formal black and white, nearing middle age, and a slender girl in a lemon evening-gown. The man was bald, pop-eyed, respectably neurotic in the essentially New Yorkish meaning of the phrase. The girl was a brunette with a mannish bob and a sleekly locked, gleaming, shallowly confident face slowly opening under the gin—a Jewish stenographer living with her parents on Fordham Road and enjoying the thrill of juggling two worlds, without serious collision, before she drove herself into the marriage test.

At the right table an entirely different couple sat—a middle-aged actress and her youthful gigolo. The woman had the face of a slightly lob-sided doll visually praying, praying, to hold back, to forget, to make enchanted in some way, the steady decay of its curves. The boy acted too insolently for the quality to be real, and sometimes, when the woman's attention was diverted, he seemed to be quaking under the glower on his straight-nosed, tanned face. Then she would turn to him with some cajolery, some confidence, and the insolence would slip back to his face, quickly, like an actor hastening to the rehearsal of a part never quite memorized.

The four at the table fronting Mona were laughing, quarreling, drooling without end and nearing the last stage of drunkenness—two young salesmen and their "steadies." One of the men, in a pepper suit, was tall and pathetic-faced—a dyed-in-the-wool amateur wisecracker—while his friend in black serge was much shorter, with a blunter face, and could have been tagged instantly as "an inferiority-complex looking for a scrap," because several gulps of straight Scotch had accomplished what they usually do in such cases—convinced the lamb that he was a wild-cat.

The girls were equally ill-assorted. One was a show-girl a bit over thirty—tight-faced, careful. The other, scarcely more than twenty, could still gurgle over the deviations in her "innocence." These eight people, with the addition of Mona and Bingham, were soon to be swept into one of those flitting brawls typical of New York speak-easies, when the alcohol shouts louder than the previous lies—a bad habit which alcohol has, if it is hurriedly swallowed and if it meets with too many strong frustrations in the swallowers.

The man in black serge lurched to his feet and staggered over to Stanley.

"Hey, you ... you keep your eyes on your own girl, or I'll punch your face for you."

Stanley promptly pushed the table forward and stood up, enraged at the unfounded intrusion.

"You damn' fool ... what are you talking about?"

"Don't pull that line on me."

"Oh, no? Well, I'll pull a lot more than a line if you don't get back to your table."

At this moment the middle-aged actress turned and cuffed Mona across the mouth. Mona, who had been flipping disdainful side-glances at the gigolo, rubbed her lips and glared at the other woman.

"What did you hit *me* for?"

"Oh, *don't* you know?"

"I think you're crazy. I don't even know who you are."

"You'll find out who *I* am, if I see you nudging his elbow again."

The young gigolo seemed to be sitting on a hot coal, with all of his insolence expelled.

"Elise, you're positively ri*dic*ulous, and I wish you'd stop raising a scene."

The young Jewess was frightened and begged her escort to hurry off with her. They left the table, and just as they were about to pass the young salesman, he fell back from a blow on the cheek dealt by Stanley and accidentally knocked the middle-aged man to his knees. Scarcely more than a second later, Mona, made furious by the other woman's yelling abuse, slapped the face of her tormentor, whereupon the entire corner became a battlefield. The tall salesman rushed to the aid of his friend and the two men fought against Bingham and his suddenly acquired, middle-aged ally. The gigolo tried to intervene between Mona and the actress and then found himself pummelled by both women, while the girls from the front table, together with the young Jewess, pulled at the coats of their men and drunkenly begged them to end the fight.

The ridiculous scramble was one of alcohol's jokes on a peculiarly shaky, American pretense of sophistication—happening also in the "American Bars" of Paris and Berlin—but in the present case the violent humor lasted hardly more than a minute. Three bouncers in tuxedos arrived—flat-nosed middleweights with sad, bored faces—and the way in which they handled the situation, without even disarranging their black bow ties, was no less than a work of art. The middle-aged man had been knocked senseless and was curled under a table, and the Jewish girl had fled. One bouncer separated Mona and the actress, efficiently but without the slightest roughness, and then seized the gigolo and threw him into a corner, with the ease of one executing a forward pass with a toy football.

He joined his comrades, who had wrenched the three fighters apart from one another with the disinterested aplomb of men performing set-up exercises to the radio. Each bouncer—evading the wildly drunken blows of his man—clutched his neck and the seat of his trousers and propelled him forward with an irresistible speed, with little, revolving jerks of the knees.

Almost before Mona and Bingham could shake off the angry mists in their heads, they found themselves standing under an electric-light pole on the sidewalk. The gigolo was dragging the actress down the street, with a mixture of kisses and blows—the swirl of hatred, dependence, begrudging love more real than its own fears allowed it to believe. The two girls were shoving their men into cabs, with a shrill jumble of attacks and pleadings, while the men cursed incoherently. Bingham fixed his eyes on the speak-easy hallway and scowled. His left eye was discolored and one side of his face swollen, and his ribs ached from the impact of blows.

"Why, the dirty rats . . . handing *me* the bum's rush because a couple of god-damn' boobs jumped on me for no reason at all. I'll get up a crowd of frat men this week and we'll come down and mop the floor with them!"

The threat was sincere for the moment, though it was one which would be forgotten during the next twenty-four hours.

Mona's only casualties were scratches on her neck and temples and a face reddened by slaps. To herself, she was achieving the difficult feat of standing in the middle of an earthquake. The sidewalk tried to rise and strike her face. The street lights, automobile headlights, were doing a foxtrot to the unholy music of sirens, back-fires. The people on the street were hopping, whirling, and then senselessly crawling, with faces as meaningless as brightly distorted pulp, and without one figment of logical imminence. Then, suddenly, she spied Emil Sperling's head as it dodged in and out of the chaotic traffic and escaped collisions always by a hair's breadth.

Despite the absence of a body, the head was not a whit grotesque but seemed to be, rather, a moving, human planet sufficient to itself. The face on the head was gentle, pained, unexpectant, and its eyes were continually fastened on Mona, inquisitively but without reproach. Abruptly, the head disappeared and the street rocked more slowly. The disappearance loosened a transformation. Every second of this night since her disgusted exit from Emil's room became pointless and flaccid—a commonplace spreading itself out to peacefully wriggling or violent moments of equal smallness. Two selves had contended for her flesh without a victory for either side, and a shiver from her soul was watching the antics and wiles of alcohol.... Bingham spoke again.

"Come on, brace up, kid. Let's forget about it. The whole damn' thing doesn't amount to a grease-spot ... sure it doesn't."

Mona stared at him with a blurred but glacial detachment.

"You're a cripple but you don't *look* like one."

"I'm *what?*"

"A cripple ... lousy old, dirty old, sweet old, young ... cripple!"

"Say, what are you talking about—have you gone nuts, dear?"

She stared at him, almost without recognition.

"Leave me alone, leave me *alone*—I haven't even been near you all night, and I'm not going near you either and I don't care *what* you say."

A cab halted at the curb directly in front of Mona—the practice of New York hackmen always attempting to foist themselves on well-dressed, seemingly easy, drunken fares. Mona opened the door and stumbled into the cab. Bingham was enraged and trying to kill his anger with a hazily humorous tolerance toward a drunken woman out of her mind. As he began to follow her into the cab, she spoke loudly.

"Get away from me . . . didn't I tell you I wasn't with you?"

The hackman, an Italian with a darkly dirty face and shifty eyes, looked at Bingham with a cold uncertainty, thinking that the other might possibly be a stranger attempting to take advantage of an inebriated girl. Stanley drew himself back to the sidewalk—frowning murderously in the throes of a pride exaggerated by whisky. If she had merely attacked him, he would not have objected overmuch, but to pretend not to know him and place him in danger of being arrested . . . by God, that was too much!

"Say . . . you can go straight to hell for all I care!"

The cab darted off and he stood without moving, watching it as it faded into the traffic. He was angry, sick of himself, swearing that he would never again trust a woman and knowing that the resolve would not be kept, and respecting the mystery in Mona's behavior, and longing to hit another man, to relieve his feelings—the elusive turbulence of human motives never more than momentarily clear to themselves before the next betraying falsity.

II

Alicia was standing with Tommy Burger in the spiritless, dimly lit hallway of her apartment house, in front of the first flight of stairs. She had just returned from "El Torado," a night club with high prices, poor food and employees, entertainers—in the black, yellow and scarlet costumes of Spain—recruited from Hoboken, Canarsie and Harlem, and therefore a rendezvous adored by New York sophisticates wearing invisible knee-pants and bibs. Alicia was tired, hesitant. She knew that Burger wanted to accompany her to the flat upstairs, that he was surfacely controlled and yet on edge with a desire largely deferred throughout the night, but much more determined now, under the push of liquor. She hesitated because her own emotions were rising and dying too quickly to be tagged or segregated—temporarily. She had been drinking too—more moderately than Burger—and his natural, sexual ability to move her had become stronger without unnerving her, but the mutters and spurts of other feelings insisted upon interfering. "Oh, how I wish *Joe* were here! I don't—he can go hang himself for all I care . . . but Joe's so much more than just a physical kick, and oh, I'm ashamed, and I can't help myself, and I'll let you hurt me and I'll like it and I'll hate myself for it, and . . . I don't want to think of the rest . . . but Joe's so much more than all that, and then . . . oh, why did I, what am I, just a *rug* for a strong, good-looking . . . yes, ring me up Monday, I'll see . . . I love Joe's ways, his nutty, dear old ways, and what he's thinking about, and how I never can tell whether the grin on his face is sincere or insincere, and I suppose I love him because I'll *die* trying to find out . . . because when I love anyone I know just enough about him to know how little I know and how crazy I am to know more . . . and when I have Joe, I throw myself out and slide down to earth again, very slowly, like on a shooting-star, oh . . . changing its mind and going slower . . . it's too difficult to describe it.

"Oh, yes? Well, goodness only knows what Mister Rosenbaum is doing with *lovely* Anna Stephens this very minute—red-heads seem to have a fatal charm for him. Oh, forget about him. You'll love at least three or four other men before you die, and . . . I don't like roses made of candy—I'd rather smell real ones."

Simple words torn from her mind, fiercely inadequate words trying to translate far less simple emotions into pride, relief, decision, censure, and achieving no more than the stumble and hint of wordless insufficiencies.

Alicia and Burger had been silent for over a minute now—the silence in which a man and a woman consciously turned over all of the possible sounds and wondered why they needed to be uttered. Alicia spoke first.

"I'd ask you up, Tommy, but Mona may have come home and if she has..."

"If she has... what?"

"Well, if she's asleep we might wake her up, and even if she isn't, we wouldn't have a bit of privacy."

"Oh, why don't you quit stalling, Alicia? You know damn' well you and she mind your own business and lead your own lives, or you couldn't last a minute together...."

"Oh, I know, but..."

"Listen, you don't need to stall with *me*. I don't expect anything from a girl just because I've taken her out. I'm not a punk—but I'm not a fool either, not too much of one anyway. If you want to drop the affair, come out with it, chick, and if you don't want to... well, you know the answer."

Alicia liked his frankness and suddenly felt that she was acting like an evasively inexperienced high-school girl, without profit to herself or Burger. If she didn't take the utterly physical escape and postponement tonight, would she be any better off when the daylight came?

"Oh, I'm an idiot, Tommy, but at least I'm reasonably aware of it."

She grasped his hand with a tacit invitation and they ascended the stairs, halting at each landing to kiss each other. After they had entered the flat, Alicia made a quick search and discovered that Mona had not returned. She stepped back to the front room where

Burger was sitting in an armchair beside one of the two windows directly above the street.

"I can't imagine what on earth's keeping that kid. She left here just a little before nine with a new friend of hers, a crippled boy. I don't know why she hasn't come back, unless..."

"Well, what's wrong with a crippled man, if he isn't paralyzed?"

"Tommy, you've got a sense of humor like... like, oh, like a dirty window-pane that needs washing. But this kid she went out with—he certainly *was* interesting. He's some kind of an artist, I think, and he can say more in less words than anybody I've ever heard."

"Oh, a high-brow... I see. Your girl-friend's getting classy, isn't she?"

Alicia had stretched herself on the square couch, with a red pillow under her head, and she gave him a mildly reproving glance.

"Well, your forehead could stand an inch or two more, and I don't mean a swelled head either."

More happily warmed by the liquor now, Burger tried to be heavily tolerant.

"Oh, let up on me... old sweet. I wasn't making any cracks. I've got lots of respect for a real artist, but I don't care for the ones with fuzzy hair and a big line of phoney gab."

Alicia became a bit more thoughtful, instinctively fighting, for the moment, against the careless dancings in her blood.

"Phoney, phoney... oh, boloney. It isn't always phoney, Tommy, just because *you* can't understand it."

Burger had seated himself on the couch and was leaning back on his elbow. He was lenient and not particularly concerned.

"Maybe you're right. I don't know. I'm only an automobile salesman, but believe me, any man who can sell cars in times like *these* ought to be able to back an intellectual off the map!"

Alicia's expression was lightly impatient, not quite a grimace, and they remained silent for a short while, teasing their own desires.

Burger was a stocky man, immaculate in his blue serge and white linen. He was one of those men, whose naked portrait in words was always "cleverly objectified but unconvincing" to the "higher" critics of his time, because they were loath to face his actualities. He was capable of robbery, assault and even murder, but, like the civilization responsible for him—which was also capable of these motives and acts—he had blindfolded his mind and heart with scores of explanations, repentances, purgings and perjuries, to hide his animal impulses from his own vision. In point of ethics, he was no better, or worse, than two million other men and women in New York City. He could extract a conscious thrill from giving a quarter to a begging man, after he himself had finished one of those innumerable, legal swindles known as business deals. It was also within him to use his fists on any man who stood in the way of his sexual desires, and in such a situation—with several drinks under his belt—even murder was not an impossibility.

He was not without softer whims and descensions, but sentimentality was decidedly a luxury to him—reserved mostly for those women who failed to oppose him, and simulated, in part, for the others. Eventually, he would rise to be one of the officials of his concern, unless some crime of passion, leading to a jail term, tripped his progress. He was thirty-two now, and he had a generally flat face with a stiff mouth, deeply set, intense eyes and brown hair.

With her own black hair straggling upon the red pillow and her flexible mouth widely parted, the sight of Alicia became a match struck against Burger's eyes. She was wearing a gray and orchid evening dress, scant and tight around her slim-slender body. He attempted another flippant comment but stopped in the middle of it, with all the words within him turned abruptly to a burning gibberish. Sliding back on the couch, he was caught, swung, within the old fury of sensual emotions—that fury which may be an ordinary jungle to its own reiterations or an inwardly delicate, clarifying flight from all of the seeming averages, all of the drab penalties and dull deceits of life on this world. To Burger, it was scarcely more than a victory of nerves—a largely frantic compensation for previous hours of restraint.

He kissed her face and mouth with the gusto of a prize-fighter unconsciously caressing his opponent. Pouncing on her body, his fingers had a clumsy mania, which sometimes, becoming aware of itself, subsided to an almost deliberate cruelty. Alicia felt repulsed, overpowered, surfacely aroused and yet self-reviling. She was, for the most part, motionless, with now and then a feeble effort to ward off his hands. He was fumbling with her dress, in the attempt to remove it, when the doorbell sounded. Alicia recognized the signal which she and Joe had once agreed upon—three short rings, a pause, and then a long ring. A bell pealed soundlessly in her heart. The sexual instigations of such an intimate situation could not be immediately banished, but Burger became now only a grossly pleasant intrusion upon her more imperative contingencies, longings, and even the pleasure was weakening, anxious to destroy itself before Rosenbaum's appearance. She jerked herself upward so irresistibly that Burger, in spite of his strength, was partly thrown aside.

"Oh, let it go—don't answer it—" Burger was surly now.

Thinking quickly, she decided upon a subterfuge, on the bare chance that, otherwise, Burger might seek to prevent her from walking to the door. True, it would be like a silly movie stunt, if he did, but . . . a girl could never tell about men.

"Maybe it's Mona—she may have forgotten her key."

"Well, you can call through the door and find out—" Burger released her, grudgingly.

She stumbled to her feet and hastily rearranged, smoothed down, her dress before she walked to the door. When she opened it, Rosenbaum was facing her. Though he never drank to the point where he might lose his balance and judgment completely, he had swallowed enough on this night to make himself intemperate, close to morbidity. He looked at Alicia with a mournful pretense of ease. Fiddling with the shoulder-straps of her dress, she was flustered, a little fearful, and yet far more distressedly happy than she had been during the previous few minutes.

"Hello . . . Josie boy."

"Hello yourself. What are you so nervous about? Entertaining somebody?"

"Yes, but come in . . . please."

"You're sure I won't be interrupting?"

"Oh, don't be a sil'—" She clutched one of the sleeves of his coat and half pulled him through the doorway.

Burger had risen from the couch. He had met Rosenbaum once, in the latter's speak-easy, and knew through hearsay that Alicia and Rosenbaum had been lovers, but he had imagined that the connection was permanently severed. He was furious at Alicia for admitting the other man and thus implying that the previous half hour had by no means overwhelmed her, and he was also determined to vanquish the intruder, but his antagonism, for the time being, could not decide upon any ready expression. Even his temper, his lack of scruples, realized that it would not be precisely an adult gesture to leap instantly upon a man who had been intimate with a woman and had entered the room through her own invitation.

Alicia, standing between the two men, affected a brightness which she could not quite carry off.

"I won't have to introduce you two boys"—she turned to Burger— "You met Joe about a month ago... don't you remember?"

"Sure. Hello, Rosenbaum. How are you?" Burger's words were transparently forced.

"Pretty good... everything considered—" Rosenbaum looked at the other man with a genuine amusement. He was at that moment struck by the futility of all jealousies, though his own jealousy refused to die and waited for the amusement to expend itself.

Burger was certain that the words "everything considered" had held a double meaning—a sly challenge—and he clenched one hand, involuntarily, and then loosened it. Let him ride for a while—the Jew punk.

"Glad to see you're *healthy* anyway."

"Yes, I usually take good care of that—" Rosenbaum smiled ever so slightly.

Alicia, darting around the room, felt jumpy, despairing, incensed at herself. Had Joe noticed all the wrinkles in her dress? Would Burger leave peacefully—would a rooster swim the Atlantic? Would Joe and Burger try to out-stay each other and make it even more ghastly for her? Oh, why did she and Joe quarrel, and make up, and tear each other's hearts out again, and make up again, and... why did they run to other people, snatch at the lowest kind of dope and then come walking back with their arms held out, their heads hanging down?

"What's the old hip-pocket weighing tonight, Joe? Honest, I think I'll perish if I don't have another drink."

"One pint of Scotch—the kind I *don't* serve to the customers—" Joe, with an elbow on the mantelpiece, grinned darkly.

"Say, if you're not a tank you'll do until a real one rolls along—" Burger, pacing before the windows, turned and regarded Alicia with a proprietor's sneer, which he sought to make humorous.

"I'll never be able to compete with *you*. Slip me the ammunition, Joe—" Alicia tossed her head, aching with every ounce of her body to manufacture a queen-like gaiety, as she approached Rosenbaum. He handed her a monogrammed silver flask and she disappeared into the kitchenette to mix the drinks.

"Can I help you, old kid?" Rosenbaum raised his voice.

"Help me? Why, listen . . . I'm going to apply for a bartender's job at your speak' next week—"

Alicia's words floated back, quivering as they strained to be merry, at ease. Joe and Burger glanced at each other with varying attitudes. Joe was unfriendly but undecided, attempting to rally his idea of sophistication, to take on the burden of a relative impersonality, despite all of the hastier counsels springing from the liquor within him. In his estimation Burger was a commonplace, fairly cunning man, to whom most of life was a business game, women included, unless he was literally *sugared* into softness, or the prize resisted all of his stratagems—a variant among a general class of men, who were frequent visitors at Rosenbaum's speak-easy, in the latter's perception. All of them sought to be rough-shod bosses—when the booze peeled off their fake manners, and often, even when they were sober—because, down at the last bottom, they were so damn' small to themselves and they had to deny, forget the smallness, no matter what the cost might be. He, Rosenbaum, could be vicious and petty, too, but he fought against it, struggled to relegate it to a degree where it existed largely as a self-defense against even worse men, but *they* never did. As far as Alicia was concerned, if she made it clear that she preferred Burger—for this night, or longer—

Mister Joseph Rosenbaum would barely manage to restrain his fists and make a quick exit, but if her attitude proved to be entirely different, the other gentleman had better grab his hat and depart. God, he was in no position to criticize *her*—with another woman's body pressed against him on the previous night.

Burger, on the other hand, looked upon Rosenbaum as a possibly yellow, politely underworldish Jew—not quite as offensive and showy as most members of his race but a Jew nevertheless and a man seeking to retain his hold on Alicia because he derived an unctuous satisfaction from keeping women at his feet, regardless of whether he was faithful to them or not. Rosenbaum wanted to be a supreme boss, like other men, but he was clever enough to smear it with soft-soap, give other people, especially women, the impression that he was fairness personified—a slippery fellow whose conceit could only be taken out of him by direct measures. Such men even pretended to be idealists at times, to be marvels of generosity, but when it came to a show-down they were looking out for themselves, first and last. Burger also told himself that—while he was not in love with Alicia—she was nevertheless highly pleasant and still unexhausted, to him, and therefore "worth fighting for."

Sitting on a corner of the couch, he talked briefly to Rosenbaum.

"How's business going at your speak'?"

"Nothing to brag about."

"Well, if you'd stop cutting your rye and buying needled beer, things might pick up."

Rosenbaum smiled, frigidly, at the seemingly unmistakable effort to provoke his temper.

"Come down and run the place some night—you seem to know so much about it."

Burger himself could not resist the cold flit of a smile—leave it to a smooth Jew every time.

Alicia tripped in with a tray bearing the highballs and both men strode forward to take it from her. Alicia was nervous, and, in turning, she knocked the bottom of the tray upward, with one of her elbows, while Rosenbaum's fingers were still trying to balance it. Burger had been reaching for the tray also, and most of the spilling liquid drenched his vest and trousers, and his shoes were spattered with broken glass. The ill-will between two men, never quite logical, even to itself, frequently needs only a trivial accident to make it childishly active, and when it occurs in a jealous blaze of alcohol, the sophistication of these men—always precarious or fictitious—finds itself unable to regain its balance.

Alicia surveyed the mess on the floor with an absurdly mournful intensity.

"Oh, I'm terribly, *terribly* sorry. I would act like an awkward cow, wouldn't I?"

Burger, sloshing the liquid from his trousers, glared up at Rosenbaum. "It wasn't your fault, Alicia. If that fool had held on to the tray, the whole thing wouldn't have happened?"

Rosenbaum's sallow face tightened and his thin lips drew near to a snarl.

"Say . . . be a little more careful with your language."

"Sure . . . I'll be as careful as you were with your paws."

"You'll be a damn' sight more careful, unless you're looking for something."

"Maybe I am. What of it? "

Alicia became agitated, persuading herself that she was frightened, that she wanted to check the quarrel, and yet hoping that Joe would not retreat because—deep within her—he was still almost an emotional idol and she resented the insults which had been given to him. She curved a hand on Rosenbaum's nearest arm and spoke before he could answer Burger.

"Joe, I want you to stop it this minute. It's all too ridiculous. You're both acting *just* like a couple of school kids!"

"Keep out of this, Alicia—" Rosenbaum pushed her away, roughly.

His brown eyes were concentrated on Burger and they were almost alertly impersonal, in spite of their anger, while Burger showed a more ordinary savagery. It was the contrast between a partial and a complete absence of thought.

"So, you're looking for something, are you?"

"Yes . . . I'm looking to break your face in for you."

"Well, come on downstairs and try to break it in there."

"Oh, yes? What's wrong with *this* place—you Jew-kike?"

The men lashed out almost simultaneously. Rosenbaum connected with a right hook to the jaw. Burger swung a low left to Joe's stomach. Gasping for a moment, and enraged at the blow, Joe drove two quick thrusts to his opponent's chest. Burger countered with a smash on the nose. Joe feinted with his right and missed with a left swing, Burger clinched and then tried another drive to the groin, but Joe side-stepped. Burger ripped in a hard left to the mouth and Joe staggered back. Burger tried to follow his advantage, with a haymaker swung from the hip, but Joe ducked and responded with two left jabs to Burger's face. Burger was stronger but Joe was the better boxer. Burger unleashed a round-house right but Joe blocked it and landed a hard right of his own on the side of Burger's neck.

Up to this point Alicia had watched the fight with a tangle of wincing and elated emotions—hating and shamefacedly relishing the fact that she was an uninjured spectator—but when, for the first time, she caught sight of the blood dripping from Rosenbaum's face, she felt herself gripped by a frantic desire to protect him. Hurrying forward, she crossed her arms around Joe's neck and, turning her head sidewise, screamed at Burger, who was standing close by with his fists raised.

"Get out of here . . . get out. You're nothing but a dirty rat and you know it. I'd never have let you come near me if I hadn't been drunk and miserable. Oh, get out of here . . . I never want to *see* you again."

With her last words half smothered by a fit of weeping, she pressed her head against Rosenbaum's chest and her knees began to sag, forcing him to place his hands under her armpits to keep her from sliding to the floor. Within this hysteria, all of the guiltiness, the plagued insignificance, the unrecognized self-dislike in her being, theatricalized by alcohol, staged a drama of relieving noise, to become wildly righteous to itself. Burger stared at her with an anger slowly hypnotized against its will. The blood-lust in him had been partly slaked by the impact of blows given and received. His hands loosened and he began to feel ludicrous to himself—a feeling which all of his surliness could not quite dismiss. In his code, a man jealously fought over a woman only when he saw some prospect of gaining, retaining her, or when she had pledged herself as his wife, his fiancée, his definite mistress, and his precious "honor" was therefore at stake, but . . . what did *this* woman mean to him except a common bundle possessed on two nights and now heaping insults upon him because she wanted to impress the man who paid her bills? This lousy Jew was probably in love with her—taking it on the face for a girl who cheated on him right and left . . . the stupid kike.

Wiping the sweat from his face, Burger walked to the card table and picked up his gray hat. Rosenbaum was supporting Alicia, patting her on the back and trying to persuade her to stop crying.

Burger looked at Joe with a superior scowl.

"I'll call it quits for tonight—it isn't even a good joke to *me*—but I'll say one thing... any man who fights over her is a prize jackass!"

"I'm not interested in anything *you* think—" Rosenbaum returned the scowl, more calmly.

"All right—go ahead. Send me a wire when you're ready for the funeral arrangements—" Burger turned and strode out of the room, banging the door behind him.

Slowly Alicia's weeping ended, and now she felt hollowed out, scarcely knowing whether she was oppressed or relieved. Her emotions were temporarily exhausted, unable to glimpse more than the confusion of their presence. Kissing Joe's mouth, half-heartedly, she slipped from his arms and attempted to revive herself, make herself steadier with little, simple tasks—stanching the blood from his nose, dabbing iodine on one of his cheeks, under the eye, and brushing the broken, crunched glass into a dustpan.

Rosenbaum threw himself on the couch, stared up at the ceiling. His mood was involved almost beyond its own cognizance—mournful, futile to itself, and thronged with indecisions, spent questions. Sometimes it seemed to him that life was simply one, unrewarded fight—one host of enmities clawing their way to small ends—forever discounted, side-tracked, by flitting harmonies, flatteries, but one sordid fight nevertheless. He had attended fashionable soirées, polite business conferences and glittering balls crowded with diplomats in spangled attire, where men and women had shown—by a twist of the eye, an involuntary jerk of the hand—that they were longing to pulverize one another under all of the amenities, the physical restraint. Now, he was moving in another world where the cheap fight was inclined to be more open, plainer and more obvious to itself, and less dependent upon wordy maneuvers—the only differences. Burger was no better, or worse, than millions of others.

The immediate question was, as always, Alicia McCulley—a girl whom he could not drive out of his blood, a girl who could be so damn' petty and, at other times, so utterly selfless that he was forced to change his opinion of her six times a night. His opinion? What in hell did that matter? When a man loved a woman, his reasons were beyond his own comprehension because love and clear thinking were absolutely alien to each other. He could spy a hundred factors to like, or dislike, but they were never the actual inceptions. Love was neither a lie nor the truth. It was a heedless, mesmerized need for the exact kind of excitement . . . tender illusions—stress and elusiveness . . . which seemed to run through a woman's words, the movements of her body, the expressions on her face and the entirety of her nature. He told himself that he would have loved Alicia if she had been an ordinary street-angler and that it was equally inevitable that he should always fight against this love, always hope to kill it. It might die tomorrow and it might last for years—who in hell ever knew?

Alicia was resting beside him on the couch now. Their faces were turned toward each other, half shadowed by the dim light from the orange-shaded lamp on the card-table near the center of the room.

"I suppose you think I'm a low-down trouble-maker, Joe. . . . Maybe I am."

"Oh, what's the use of calling yourself names? That doesn't change anything?"

"But I'm sick and tired of myself. I can't seem to get any grip on things."

"You might drink a little less, and see what happens."

"*That* from *you*—oh, Joe, dear . . . you're a card."

"I may be one at that. I feel exactly like the ace of spades . . . but

I meant what I said just the same. It's all right to drink when you're happy, or just bored with everything, but don't try it when you've got the jim-jams—it never works then."

"But that's just the time a person *wants* to drink. Joe, I've got to pull myself together. We simply can't go on like this . . . quarrelling, and hurting each other, and getting into all sorts of messes."

"The only messes I see are the ones you make yourself. You won't marry me . . . you won't even live with me . . . and then, to cap it all, you throw yourself at a man like Burger. I came up here tonight to have it out with you, once and for all. If I'm not the main thing in your life, for Christ's sake tell me . . . and you'll never see me again."

"But you *are*, Joe. If you'd only stop fuming and getting into rages because I won't live with you, there'd be absolutely nothing left to quarrel about."

"Nothing except a regiment."

"Don't exaggerate, dear."

"I'm not, but that isn't the point. We can't stay peaceful with each other and it seems we can't stay away from each other. Something's got to be done about it."

"What would *you* suggest—you're so terribly wise, aren't you?"

"Yes, we're both fools, but I'd suggest that you make up your mind and stick to it. If you refuse to live with me, then you can confine yourself to men like Burger, and I'll fade out of the picture. That's why I came up tonight. It's going to be decided this time, one way or the other."

"That's beautiful, Joe. Now you'll be able to go back to your darling Anna Stephens."

"I'd be a damn' sight better off, if I did. That girl would tear the skin off her body, if she knew I needed it . . . but I suppose that's why

I can't love her. I must have a carpet hidden in me *somewhere*, or I wouldn't be so damn' anxious to have you walk on me."

"Will you please tell me how I'm walking on you? I'm willing to be with you almost every night... gladly... but I want to live *alone*. I can't bear the idea of being tied down to a man, no matter how much I love him. It's so hard to explain, Joe, but... I can be a slave to a man when I know I'm absolutely free, in every way, but when I don't know it... then I feel miserable and rebellious."

An unwilling understanding loosened his thin lips, swollen by Burger's knuckles, but his needs were too strong to allow it to dominate him. He slipped from the couch and stepped slowly around the table, to ease his tension, if only a hair's breadth.

"I'm not entirely bundled up in myself—I know how you feel—but there's always a way out of it. I'll rent a duplex apartment—give you one whole floor to yourself—and you can come and go as you please. I won't even carry *one* key to your part of it."

She looked at him with a stubborn, curdled, admiring pity and refusal torn from all of the contradictory depths of her young egotism.

"You're a brick, Joe... and I know I don't deserve you... but I just can't make myself do it. It isn't only the flat problem—it's all the little things, too... calling you on the 'phone... wondering whether I'll catch you in... and then working over-time and just about breaking my silly neck to meet you without being too late... oh, loads and *loads* of things."

Sprawling in an arm-chair beside the table, Joe was enormously angry again.

"Well, how about my side of it? Do you think I like to sneak out of here, about seven in the morning, feeling like a ton of coal? Do you think I like to wake up and take in the empty walls, with nothing to hug but the pillow you've been sleeping on? Do you think I'm crazy about making love to you, with another woman sleeping in the same flat? Why, it's impossible to be happy under such conditions. We're not living naturally—that's the trouble."

"But Joe, dear ... it's not going to be forever. If we're still together six months from now, I'll be so dependent on you I'll *have* to give in—I won't be able to help it—and if we're *not* ... then there's nothing to talk about."

"No, nothing except yourself. I've always known I was pretty selfish but you're just about half a mile ahead of *me*."

He lifted his coat from the chair, drew his arms into the sleeves and picked up his black slouch hat. When he had reached the door, Alicia sprang from the couch and ran to him.

"Joe, please don't go! I couldn't stand it, Joe—I'd murder myself. Oh, Joe! Joe . . . try to understand me, won't you? Give me just another month before I decide ... please, dear. I'm so torn between things I don't know my head from my heels any more!"

She plaited her arms behind his shoulders and kissed every part of his face, lingering particularly on his eyes and cheeks, and her mouth was a bittersweet, unnerving mixture of pain and coercion to him. Her shoulder-straps had fallen and one of her bare breasts, jammed against his chest, was whisky and sugar crystallized in an overwhelming sense of touch. All of the words people pour out to one another—the redundant, inarticulate or glibly protective words—became cunningly veiled frauds or zeroes to him. Only a poet could change words to nimble symptoms of reality, but, to other people, they could never be more than desperate lines of defense endlessly concealing the thousands of motives, which were often secrets even to themselves—the malices, jealousies, sacrifices and tender escapes,, shifting into one another, often with only a flitting assumption of identity.

These thoughts and feelings visited him, almost wordlessly, as he cupped Alicia's breasts in the palms of his hands, and stroked her torso and hips, and gave his lips to the curiously obvious mystery of her mouth—a mystery because it could never be assimilated and yet barely evaded such a completeness.

They heard the rattle of a key and separated, unwillingly. Mona pitched herself into the room, slamming the door behind her. Her blonde hair had tumbled over her forehead and her hat was awry. Her wide lips were open and distressed, like those of a clown suddenly forced to realize his own seriousness, without quite being able to achieve it, and the scratches on one side of her face stood out against the milky-white skin. Never having known Mona to drink herself to such an oblivion, Alicia was humorously surprised and solicitous.

As Mona leaned against one of the short walls jutting between the two rooms, Alicia stepped forward and tenderly raised Mona's chin.

"My *dear* . . . what on earth has happened to you? You look like a total *wreck*—I've never *seen* you this way before . . . I'm frightened. D'you hear me, dear? What happened? Did anyone do something wrong to you?"

Mona smiled, with a bleary remoteness.

"I'm a cripple . . . everybody's cripple . . . s'funny too, but I just found it out."

She lurched forward, with her words reduced to a mumble, and disappeared behind the portières. Alicia and Rosenbaum stared after her—amused, concerned and completely unable to understand.

Chapter Three

I

MIGUEL ROMALOS, nicknamed Meekie, lived in the dirtier and less respectable part of Columbia Heights, one short block away from the foot of Atlantic Avenue—that lower part of Brooklyn hemmed between the shadows of two great bridges and confronted, across the turbid sweep of the East River, by the caterpillar piers and the uplifted, gray talons of Manhattan's downtown district. The upper stretch of Columbia Heights was a laughable medley—politely seedy rooming-houses, tall hotels with a slightly off-color swank, former mansions, some of them boarded up, with high-walled rear gardens and brassily remodeled apartment-houses, private tennis-courts and somnolent shops, all of them jumbled together and typical of a run-down section, once fashionable and now desperately mending a few of the tears in its former finery.

However, in the neighborhood where Meekie dwelt, the mercenary real-estate revivals, always masquerading as civic improvements, had given up in despair. The buildings were little more than tenement houses—three- and four-story cubes and slabs with the red and brown paint peeling from their bricks and with streaks of rust on the iron fire escapes and street railings. Even on the sunny wideness of Atlantic Avenue, a New Yorkish flirtation was going on between the ash-cans on the sidewalks and the bedquilts hanging for an airing from the open windows. The stores were small glooms and the lunch rooms grease specks, in all the sores and apathies of trade, human existence, which New York City disowned so carefully with the brave show and bustle of its major thoroughfares.

The little street-end where Meekie lived was hardly a stone's fling from the ship masts, the ferries, the coal and lumber yards on the river-front, and huge, pounding trucks continually tore up and down beneath his flat. He stayed with his father in two dark rooms and a kitchen. Sometimes a married sister came over to cook their meals. A brother of Meekie, a saxophone tooter, lived in Manhattan and was largely indifferent to his family, and a young sister, the remaining child, had disappeared into one of the flesh-selling haunts of Harlem. The mother had died six years before. Ramon, the father, worked in an adjacent lumber yard—piling and loading boards, ten hours a day. Meekie was clerking in a hardware store now—a job which he called "easy meat," though it frequently involved the lifting and unpacking of heavy barrels and crates. He had attended high school through the insistence of his mother, who had wanted her favorite child to be "a beeg, beeg man some day." After her death, during his second year at high school, he ran off and joined the crew of a freighter bound for a South American port. A year of this tough, cramped, rip-snorting life followed and then he deserted the ship and became, in turn, a porter, a shovel-swinger, a truck-pusher, a hobo and a janitor's assistant.

Then an accident brought his father a strained back, and Meekie returned to Columbia Heights—the region where he had been born and raised—to help the married sister in nursing the old man. Meekie liked Ramon, but the liking was disrespectful, roughly compassionate, growling. He regarded Ramon as an old fool, blind to his own high-handed spites, but he admired Ramon's refusal to accept favors—the morose independence which made the father continue to strain his weakened muscles at the age of fifty-seven—and he was also responsive to the latter's moments of gruff wit, man-like boisterousness under whisky or wine.

Meekie was twenty-five now, and all of the slam-bang, captious, instantly guffawing and enslaved elements in his heart and mind had experienced the abrupt beginning of a revolutionary change. Two months earlier they had crashed into a girl named Ena Monteith, who had been introduced to Meekie by a mutual acquaintance in the ribald sloppiness of an Italian speak' on Bleecker Street. Crashed was not an exaggeration, for Ena had proved to be an extraordinary girl to Meekie. She represented the first out-and-out, youthful vagabond he had ever encountered in the female sex. He had observed feminine bums before, on the benches of Bryant and Madison Square Parks, but they had always been at the end of middle age, elderly or decrepit—women with coarse, beaten faces, reddish noses and little education, cringing underneath the drab odds and ends which they wore.

Ena was approaching twenty-six—a short, deliriously plump firebrand of a girl, with unconfined, blonde hair flowing almost to her waist. She scorned head-gear of any kind, and snow and rain often made a natural wreath for her head, as she walked down the streets of New York, while vapidly normal passers-by often stopped to stare, giggle, make ridiculing comments to one another. She had a small, stub-nosed, green-eyed face with even, white teeth and a tinily pugnacious chin. She wore original dresses, peasant costumes cut and sewed by her own hands, with long, wide skirts touching her sandalled feet, and high kirtles and waists, and old-silver jewelry, and in the winter she could always be seen in a long, plain black cape fastened by one button over her bosom. Her belongings were scattered over New York City—a basement in Jackson Heights, a garret in Greenwich Village, a closet in a Bronx apartment—and she was continually visiting friends and acquaintances to procure the articles which she needed. Her abodes were never fixed and often determined by the happenings of each night. Sometimes she lived with different men for periods varying from three days to a month. At other times she remained physically aloof from men for months, if she failed to meet any man who was attractive to her wild, difficult, imaginative desires, and also responsive to her.

Often she bummed a night's lodging from some woman, met for the first time, or some man, to whom she denied her body, and in the summer time she frequently slept, during the early morning hours, on a bench in one of the squares and parks, or sat there, greeting the dawn with a male friend. Esthetic dancing was the disorderly and yet impulsively disciplined breath of her existence and she practiced her dances, day after day, in studios loaned for an afternoon by artist friends, for whom she posed—occasionally—to earn a few dollars. She had won scholarships in the schools of Doris Humphrey and Mary Wigman, but had always wound up by quarreling with the fixed techniques of these places, and she had also held small recitals before audiences of friends and acquaintances.

To Meekie, she was a staggering visitation—a girl entirely without the earmarks, the hidden conservatisms, the coquettish tricks and fastidious squirms of her sex—particularly of "a good girl"— and yet neither a whore nor in any way commonly promiscuous, and, in spite of everything, a *girl* through and through. She had withheld her body from him for weeks—saying only that she was temporarily tired of sex—and then she had yielded to him, gayly, without the least invitation or supplication on his part. He had watched her repulse the overtures of scores of men, who had imagined that she must be only an eccentric "Greenwich Village tart," and yet he realized dimly that she had taken many men in her life and that she regarded morals as no more than ash-cans masquerading as divinely pure altars and waiting for basic emotions to be consumed.

Meekie had treated Ena with a joking, concealed curiosity at first, and then, after his initial date with her, he had been bewildered, angered, grudgingly respectful, and when the third meeting had passed, he began to be thoughtful and a little self-critical, floundering against walls whose existence he had never guessed before. Another two meetings and he was in love with her, in spite of all the sullen disclaimers still mumbling within him. Liking his rough-and-ready hatreds, his honest ignorances, Ena had sensed a bottom defiance within him—unknown to itself, misdirected on the top—and had proceeded to beat him away from the outward ruts of the under-dog doping himself with booze, stupid women, and fights with his fellow slaves. Knowing that Meekie had few esthetic perceptions, Ena had talked Communism to him. She was by no means implicitly a Communist herself—her intangible uncertainties were too endless for that—but she wanted Meekie to see the malodorous, glibly hidden forces ruling his life, to snarl back at them, to weep over them, to become enraged at the sufferings, the deceits and cheap sugars endlessly ladled out to the people in his general stratum of life.

The task had been difficult, but after two months of this contemptuous and yet good-natured pounding, Meekie found himself slowly altering to a mind-shaken, embryonic social rebel.

He was sitting now, in a corner pool room a few doors down from his flat. He had arranged to meet Ena at "George's Rendezvous" on the present night and was whiling away an intervening hour. Hunched on the cane-bottomed, wobbly chair, Meekie flipped through a copy of *The New Yorker* which he had picked up in a subway coach on the previous night. Various items signalled. "There's an Etonish sort of collar worshiping at the new shrine of the Higher Neck Line." "Do the creators of fashion in Paris sanction nails that are tinted or natural?" "I suppose I am getting a little bit incoherent about this book, but really, it is one of the finest things I've read in some time"—this in praise of a book entitled *Invitation to the Waltz*, dealing with the fussings, delights and fears of an English debutante attending her first society ball—and "when the judges examined the flasks of the Fort Meyer Army Team, they found them filled with Coca-Cola!"

Staring at the pages, Meekie swore and glowered to himself. An ominous smile dug into his swarthy face. Two nights before he had watched the continually shuffling bread-lines on Times Square—men with numb, furtive or stolidly hopeless faces, pressing forward, two abreast, to reach for a chunk of bread and a tin cup of coffee. During the same week, he had witnessed a rent eviction on his own block—a middle-aged woman and three children temporarily sheltered by their neighbors, with the rain falling on the small huddle of furniture standing close to the curbstone . . . and here were these suave, polite, higher racketeers pattering about polo, and the new shrine of the higher neck line, and the wonderfully written thrills and quandaries of a debutante at a ball, with only an occasional, mildly satirical smile for the tragic mess around them—all of which Meekie translated as "high-class b.s. from a bunch of clever boloneys." Tearing two pages from the magazine, he left the chair and disappeared into the rear darkness of the pool room. Emerging again, he stood beside one of the tables and watched a game for a time.

He was a trifle over medium height, with long legs and bulwarked shoulders. His skin was a lemonish brown and some people mistook him for a Negro—an imputation which still made his blood boil just a bit, in spite of Ena's laughing scorn at this reaction. Glancing idly at the pool game, he fingered the bright red tie that Ena had induced him to buy—over-riding his objection that red was no color for a man—and his broad-nosed, thick-lipped face, under the wet bush of black hair, was separate and indecisive, as it turned from one to another of the faces peering over the green baize.

God-damn' peculiar, wasn't it?' Only two months ago he had held a load of respect for some of these fellows, and even the ones he had hated or disliked—because of grudges, peeves over girls, or dough—had been pretty important, accepted, to him, but now... damned if they weren't half-wits, the whole mob, with a few of them taking advantage of the others. Whether they worked their guts out, or tried to "get it easy," they were mucks—squeezed out on all sides—"taking each other for small coin" and slamming fists and getting broke every Saturday night to make a hit with the girls they took out. Why? Because they wanted to forget that they didn't have one chance in a thousand, that they would wind up in the hoosegow or in a lousy flat, pulling their bellies out to support a wife and another kid every year or two.

Look at Pedro Carrova, with that thick smile on his pan—some kind of a district inspector for the Street Cleaning Department and tied up with the McCooey outfit. He had to "get out the votes" in his precinct, and here he was at the table, missing easy shots so he would lose the side-bet, and handing out perfectos, and yessing the other three blue in the face. And Danny Fitzgibbons whispering to the mug beside the rack—a hot tip on the fifth at Belmont...

kiss your five bucks bye-bye, you egg. And Petey Guitterez, out on parole from Elmira—he had been loving up a girl in the hallway of her place, and her old man had caught him and swung for his face, and Petey had sliced the old guy in the scrap which had followed. He'd be in jail again soon—it was like fighting against kicks in a dark room and never knowing where the next one was coming from. And Larry Krause, Louie Frenozza, Mike Salvatore, the routs, losing their money at pool, losing their girls to other fellows, working their skins off, and always having the life kidded out of them. And oily Freddy Miller, always talking about skirts and bragging that he had touched up half of the girls on both sides of the block—and the joke was that he *had*, too, because most of them needed no more than a fast line of chatter, a cabaret and a taxi ride home, before they gave up in the basement or on the roof. . . .

The pool room was heavy with rings and drifts of grayish-blue smoke. The tan plaster walls were cracked and dotted with dark-brown spots. Harshly concentrated faces gleamed under the green-shaded lights over each of the three tables, and a loud babble contended against the click of the balls, the stamping of cues. "I squeezed her fat legs and then she had the nerve to ask me . . ." "Who's a fool?" "I saw the bastard with me own eyes, chinning with a dick near the sub' entrance . . ." "I tell you, I've got the only system—play the favorite on the nose and play a long shot to show in the same race . . ." "Say, when we get through with that guy, he'll have a tomato for a nose . . ." "Aw, her old lady found out she was knocked up and she raised a stink about it . . ." "Sure, he does. He's in with a couple of clip joints and they give him a percentage on all the stews he hauls . . ." "Fifteen per, I'm telling you—that's all he gets, and he has to sweat plenty on that job . . ."

Meekie was unanimously distrusted by the pool-room hangers-on. Since he had only returned to the neighborhood a few months before, and since the gangs had changed many times during his long absences, he was a comparative stranger now to most of the present habitués. At first they had been inclined to accept him as a close-mouthed, fairly regular guy, handy with his knuckles in the one scrap of his which they had witnessed, but the past two months had reversed the verdict. He had commenced to fling back short, derisive replies to their badinage, their business overtures—not the profane, cheeky kidding, tempered by more serious attention when the intended victim showed that "his goat was tied up"—the conduct which they practiced themselves—but cutting remarks dealing with the obtuseness of their lives, in which they heard themselves referred to as "wage slaves," "swindled boobs," and "back-scratchers for all the big shots, who don't even know you're alive unless they can use you."

The result had been inevitable. They began to regard him as a rat with a swelled head, trying to show off and pretend that he was better than they were. They also looked upon him as a sorehead, shooting his mouth off because he had not been able to worm his way into the more lucrative rackets of the neighborhood. Some of them believed that he might be a lousy Red—one of those longhaired, crappy weak-sisters out to stir up trouble for their own benefit—while others held to the view that he was only a damn' fool with a screw loose in his head. Yet, up to date, they had failed to molest him because, like most of the corner mobs in New York, they were far less anxious to fight than they affected to be, unless a gang could leap on a single man, or unless one of the two contestants had a decided advantage in height and weight. However, the small explosion was always ready, waiting for some errant whim to ignite it.

The pool game at the table ended, and Meekie selected a cue

from the rack.

"Anybody want to shoot for half a buck on the side?"

Freddy Miller measured Meekie up and down with a barely covered insolence. He was a tall youth in a lurid green suit, with a high, level-bottomed vest and broadly cuffed trousers, and his flat-nosed face was cunning in a minor way—a well-buttered brutality.

"We ain't playing with you. We don't like the shape of your face, see?"

"What's that got to do with shooting a game of pool?"

"Plenty. We might have to listen to some of that cheap gas of yours."

"Oh, yeah? Well, if you can stand your own gas you're doing pretty well at that."

Freddy scowled an inch away from decision, gripping his cue and aching to swing it on Meekie's head. Louie Frenozza and Pedro Carrova walked up to Meekie, hemming him in on both sides but remaining a foot away from him. Pedro was short and fat in his dark blue worsted. A diamond solitaire pressed into one of his pudgy fingers and a Knights of Columbus emblem dangled from the thin chain across his vest. His face was jowled, smooth, spongily unscrupulous. Frenozza, on the other hand, was a watery-eyed hulk in a hand-me-down graychecked suit—easily swayed and unusually dull-witted. Carrova spoke first.

"What the hell's been eating you lately, Romalos? I hear you've been peddling a line of crap to the boys here—telling them they're not getting a square deal. What about it?"

"That's right—" Meekie leaned against the rack, with his hands in his pockets and gave Carrova an acid smile. "They're willing to let you and all the other soft-soap merchants rob them right and left, because they're not wise to themselves. But you're only a small potato yourself, Ped. The big bosses—the ones that rake in the real dough—they don't even know you're alive."

Carrova glowered but Frenozza spoke before the former could answer.

"Oh, yeah? I suppose *you're* not after the coin yourself. The hell you're not. You're sore because you ain't got brains enough to get it."

Carrova edged closer to Meekie.

"So, I'm a small potato, huh? Well, you're not even that much. You're raising a big stink because we don't want you here and we won't let you dig your fingers in the feed-bag. We're wise to your game, and what's more . . . if you don't like the way we run things you can grab a boat for Russia where you belong."

The smile on Meekie's face only deepened.

"What's the matter, Ped—aren't you going to hand me one of those dime ropes you've been slipping around here? That's too bad, Ped."

The smile and the carelessly sneering words were more corrosive to Pedro than yards of angry controversy would have been, and he was also afraid that Meekie might be impressing the boys . . . just a trifle. He turned to Freddy Miller.

"Say, are you going to let this rat here get away with talk like this?"

Miller's intense desire to "stand in" with the figure of local influence overpowered his remnants of fear, of discretion.

"No, not by a damn' sight—" He swung his right and landed a glancing blow on Meekie's temple.

In another second Meekie was battling against Miller and Frenozza—ducking, blocking and dodging between the tables, to offset the unfair odds, and occasionally planting a solid blow of his own. He tried to be cool and hopeful, but he was shaky, wildly despairing, beneath the effort, because he knew that his chance was one in a hundred and that the others were only too anxious to clip him. At this juncture, Jose Marranza, the proprietor, rushed up from the cigar-stand beside the doorway. He was an ax-jawed man over six feet tall, with a swarthy, broadly truculent face—an ex-prizefighter noted for his rough eccentricities, and a Republican precinct-leader, and the owner of much property in the neighborhood.

He shouldered his way between Meekie and Miller, prying them apart, and pushing Miller heavily against one of the tables. Then he turned to Frenozza and the other men, with his fists poised.

"Listen, you mugs . . . don't try to gang this kid while I'm around. You lay off him—the whole bunch of you. He's been giving you the low-down, that's what, and you mugs don't want to hear it, but believe me, I'm getting sick and tired of that god-damn' bunch of pick-pockets down at City Hall. Don't let Pedro pull the wool over your eyes—he gets paid for everything he's doing, and don't forget it!"

The boys were uncertain now—respecting Marranza's jeering belligerence, caught between equally sullen persuasions, and beginning to wonder what in hell they had been scrapping about. They had hated Meekie more because he dared to be different in his words, sparing in his praise, than because their patriotic haze was in any way a deeply courageous verity.

Carrova gave the proprietor a venomous look but hesitated, afraid of the other man's known eagerness to deal blows and realizing that, once more, he would have to spill the oil freely to regain the full swing of his prestige. The Republicans were powerless in that locality, but a seriously lowered vote could always send him into the discard.

Taking advantage of the lull, Meekie grabbed his hat from a

near-by chair and bolted through the doorway. He was not lacking in an average share of the unfeeling, animal momentum designated as physical courage, but he had no intention of remaining, like a lamb, for the possible slaughter. His ups and downs on ships, beside railroad tracks and in tough speak-easies had taught him that discretion was usually a shade better than a broken jaw. As he walked quickly down the streets, he was jammed between wrathful quivers and the morbid desire to laugh at himself. What in hell was the use of telling those eggs *anything*, and even if they believed a guy, what in hell could they do about it? They were all helpless, side-tracked in a hundred ways, and at the mercy of a few men whom they never even met face to face—men with thousands of cops and soldiers to carry out their orders. Rubbing his black eye, his bruised forehead, Meekie felt insignificant, sullenly hopeless. The feeling survived as he boarded a crowded subway train for Greenwich Village and "George's Rendezvous."

The time was eleven-thirty and the "Rendezvous" was nearing its first climax. The place had become immensely popular and even on the first days of the week tens of people were turned away after midnight for lack of seats. Yet it was still unrecommended and scantily noticed by the recreation magazines and papers of New York City because certain, prearranged factors, unprecedented features, entered the situation. The place was without a cover charge and minus the wardrobe-checking racket, and the minimum charges were only twenty-five cents up to Fridays and fifty during the week-end nights. In addition to these horrible omissions, the manager had been instructed to be reasonably impartial to all of the patrons, regardless of the amounts which they spent or the quality of their clothes, and he carried out the orders with a surprising lack of discrimination, in spite of the fact that he was naturally forced to become a tactful automaton. Again, the "Rendezvous" had run into the smugly New Yorkish tendency to sneer at, or ignore, any public place with the smallest pretension of a "Villagey" atmosphere.

George Damero, the main proprietor, had gathered a group of impoverished Village dancers, poets, violinists, singers and ukulele players, and hired them as entertainers, furnishing them with their meals and small salaries. He also tried to foster a spirit of informality, without encouraging it to that degree where it would have ended in a rough-house free-for-all. He was a self-centered capitalist at heart, of course, and his place was definitely commercial, but he had been shrewd enough to realize that certain people—particularly in a time of great, material depression—were out of patience with the robberies and the press-agented frauds prevailing in New York night resorts and would flock to any new hang-out possessing actual, surface innovations. As a consequence, he had been continually persecuted since the opening of his establishment several months previous. The other cabaret and night-club owners of the Village had banded together in an attempt to prevent him from securing a dancing license and at first he had been compelled to station look-outs at his entrance and "bootleg" the dances at irregular intervals, whenever these sentries anpounced that no detectives were cruising in the vicinity. Then, after he had obtained the license by paying an exorbitant sum for it, he had been visited several times by the police captain of the district, who had bellowed the old excuse concerning complaints that perverts and prostitutes were frequenting the "Rendezvous."

On top of this, he had been approached by a gang leader of the Village who had demanded protection money running into hundreds every month, and had hinted that he might "wreck the joint" if the money were not forthcoming. Damero had been able to survive these tactics only because he happened to have a lucky, surface friendship with one of the high officials in the City Government—the inevitable tribulations of any capitalist in New York City seeking to be even a moderate shade fairer, less hidebound and less predatory than the others in his specific line of business.

He strolled from table to table now, chaffing, flattering and steadily solicitous, much like the proprietors known to New York cafés and dance places before the World War and Prohibition ushered in a wise-cracking, strained, trim-the-sucker atmosphere. Damero was a heavily built Continental in black broadcloth, with saturnine eyes and an over-carnal mouth. When he stood still, his feet were always at right angles, a left-over from his service in the Austro-Hungarian navy. His partner, Ivan Polnikoff, stood just inside of the entrance, patting the white carnation which he invariably wore—a Russian Gentile with a fat, blandly superior, brown-mustached face, a considerable knowledge of art, particularly music, and excitable, unconsciously overbearing, punctilious ways. He was, at bottom, a sentimentalist trying to protect himself by imagining that he had a contempt for most human beings.

The hostesses, in vari-colored pajama outfits, were young and had the modulations and poise of that inwardly precarious lie known as physical refinement—girls whose faces were fresher, less hard and smeared than those of the usual feminine employees in New York night places. One was drawing at the Art Student's League, another was attending college, still another had once owned and conducted her own tea room in the Village, while a fourth was studying sculpture. None of them occupied the position of compulsory hostesses, but they were permitted to talk and dance with the male patrons, if they chose. Damero had a European tolerance in regard to morals and his only insistence was that the girls should not pick up men and accommodate them for money. He also prohibited another old favorite of New York hot spots—hired girls bestowing pressures and honeyed insinuations upon a patron, to induce him to spend more freely and give him the false belief that he would be made physically happy after closing time. Any waitress suspected, in either or both of these regards, was instantly dismissed by George, but he made no effort to discourage the voluntary and spontaneous attachments sometimes springing up between the girls and different male habitués. The quaint, New York custom of having the male wait on an adjacent street-corner, instead of boldly leaving with the hostess in question, failed to appeal to his sense of humor.

On this particular Saturday night, every table at the "Rendezvous" was filled and almost three hundred people sat downstairs, or in the balconies which extended over both sides of the dance floor and ended in a rectangular space at the rear. The place had been formerly a Chinese chop-suey palace in the New York grand manner and it was lavishly appointed in gold, dark blue and crimson, with green Bakelite tables and wall-panels depicting sprites in an orange sea: Leda ravished by the swan, monks rolling among the fragments of broken wine-jugs and other conventional fancies. At the beginning of each week, George used a large, combined radio and phonograph for his dancing, but on the last three nights he employed a good, second-rate, seven-piece band from Harlem, and these Negroes were now braying and thudding while tens of couples tried to avoid collisions on the floor.

When the band was resting, the entertainers held forth. The first to perform was a short, frail-bodied man just over thirty, whose clothes were neat but baggy and worn—a Village poet named Eric Beagle, who had a drooping nose, screwed-up lips, and an attitude of unconsciously arrogant meekness. His grayish-brown face was almost childishly ascetic and, despite his age, it revealed not a single mark of sexual experience. Years before the present night he had achieved a flitting prominence when one of the "seriously cultured" magazines in New York had awarded him its annual poetry prize, on the strength of a rambling, awkward, blustering poem reminiscent of Walt Whitman and entitled "Warm Evenings Have Existed in Nebraska." Since then he had trudged and drudged in a relentless obscurity, fighting against starvation, vermin in cheap rooming houses, indifference and ridicule.

He stood motionless under the spotlight, with his arms glued to his sides, and delivered his unworldly, indignant, compassionate verse in an unfortunate voice, which was nasal, rasping, rising frequently to a shriek. All of his inhibitions, his pains and disappointments avenged themselves in this roar of liberation. A party of slummers at a front table—flippantly inflated and gin-soaked—refused to listen to him and kept up a barrage of squeals, loud bandyings. George, who was standing on the band platform, hurried to the radio-microphone—a relic of the former owners—which was disconnected now but still amplified the voice. His face was drawn with anger as he glared at the offenders. "Silence ... silence, please! I wish to make an announcement. This place is not a speak-easy. This is a place for both serious and not-serious entertainment. Those who do not wish to listen can get their checks immediately, and leave. I do not want them here."

A member of the party lurched to his feet—a tall man in dark tweed, with the flushed, broadly pugnacious face of a Rotarian out to demand "his rights."

"Sa-ay, d'you mean to tell *me* you're willing to lose good, paying cust'mers just because they won't stand for this yelling fool here?"

"Yes, that is what I mean. If you do not care to listen, please pay your checks and go somewhere else."

The man turned to the other four at his table.

"Come on, folks, let's beat it out of here. Why, the god-damn' jackass! This guy must think he's God Almighty!"

The party rose and made an exit, with the over-painted women raising shrill, sarcastic remarks until the doors closed behind them. Beagle stepped to the spotlight again, and now he was grinning apologetically.

"I'm sorry I didn't listen to the people who just left. The whole thing was a sad mistake—they were the speakers and I was supposed to be the audience, but . . . would you like me to change places again? It's entirely up to you."

The grinning "modesty" kindled the approval of the audience and a scattered round of applause ensued, after which Eric plunged back to his task of flaying the surrounding ear-drums. When he had finished, the clapping was hearty, for a moment, from people who had been squirming, whispering. It was New York incarnate—the fake leniency, if not worship, toward any man who said: "Aw, I don't deserve any credit" or "I'm not so good but I'm doing my best," because such a man drew himself nearer to the beaten-down, inept, defrauded level of the spectators and made them less envious.

Beagle was followed by Jimmy Ellison, a thin middle-aged man whose baldness crept into a rear thatch of grayish-mousey hair. Ellison had the face of a reformed Mephistopheles sitting by the fireside—a long, pointed nose, pencil-thin lips, arched eyebrows, and a tiny, cutely pointed mustache. He strummed the accompaniments to his songs on a brightly decorated ukulele, made partly from a cigar-box, and sang his own creations in a flat, brittle voice. He had been a locally famous character in one of the heydays of the Village, just before Prohibition, when he had strolled from tea room to dancing place, playing and singing from a spontaneous exuberance, without expecting or accepting money, since he earned a meagre living as an illustrator and photographer. Even now, he was still under the impression that Greenwich Village existed in something more than name, in contrast to those hopeful mourners who insisted that its demise had occurred immediately after the death of "The Liberal Club" on MacDougal Street.

Standing on the floor now, he received an unbroken attention as he sang: "She's the belle of Hubert's cafet-t-teria, down on Sheridan Square, where the nuts and the bums with their sex-hysteria, patiently give her the air. She's got no home; the poor girl must roam. She domiciles anywhere. And her stockings are cotton; they're torn and they're ... uh ... declassé! ... She's the peril of Sheridan Square ... The Sultan's wives have got the hives—Allah, be merciful! The Sultan's wives have got the hives, through eating an-cho-vies and chives. The Sultan's sons, the sons-of-guns, have taken the harem's fairest ones—Fatima and Scheherezade. There will be hell! There will be, uh, ... trouble. When the old man from the war arrives, the Sultan's wives will lose their lives, from inadvertently contracting hives! Alla-ah! ... 'Come to my home in the sewer,' said the cockroach to his mate. 'Come where the air is impu-re, but the atmosphere is great!' 'N-n-n-n-no,' cried the lady-cockroach. 'I'll stay right here by the sink!' But the cook baked her up in a pudding, and put her on the blink! ... blink, blink ... blink ... bli-i-ink ... blink-blink."

At the conclusion of each song he raised the ukulele high above his head and stood with an innocently solemn look on his face. After he had been wildly applauded, he introduced a Village girl—Thelma Robinsky—a Jewess barely twenty, with a huge shock of black, curly hair and the almost curveless body of a thirteen-year-old. Her face was unSemitic, more like the steep-nosed, red-lipped, saffron-brown features of a Moorish girl. In a long black skirt, vermilion sweater, she danced to "The St. Louis Blues," with knees jerking forward, striking together, torso held straight, or barely inclining, arms close to the body and hands with stiff wrists and fingers making little, horizontal or diagonal passes. It was the convulsive interpretation of a Negress suffocated with sensuality, tortured by inexpressible pleasure and struggling against the uppermost intensities of the bondage.

Thelma was compelled to give an encore, and then she was succeeded by a tall poet with waves of black hair and a lean, pear-shaped face. He rendered a lengthy poem in jazz-music rhythms—the emotions of a creole girl and her lover, fleeing from death at the hands of a posse of "poor whites" and halting on a shaggy hilltop to embrace each other, apart from the cruelties and sentimentalities of an actual world. The poem, in style and content, was above the heads of two-thirds of the audience, but the poet, Gordon Saxby, was so fervently oblivious to his surroundings, so varied in tempo and tonal range, and so utterly allied with the characters in the piece, that he literally forced alcoholic men and women to listen to him in a dead silence. He gave way to a young violinist, Cloyd Wagner—a large-eyed, ruddy boy with an impersonal frown. Under the difficulty of playing without a piano accompaniment, Wagner slid through a fugue by Cyril Scott and a short selection from Vincent D'Indy's "Mountain Suite," and accomplished them with a competent technique and a shy approach to understanding.

The entertainment continued, free from the inevitable tap-dances, adagios, high kicks, tango teams, worldly gags and inanely tripping girls with bare legs, stomachs and half-covered breasts—omissions which would have caused great disappointment to large numbers of New York's cultured sophisticates and low-brow vulgarians so-called. The crowd at George's became noisier as the number of empty bottles grew under the tables, but some of the groups were effervescent without being boisterous. A man named Howard Grannihan was standing at the head of a table and addressing a smiling quartette. Grannihan had been a Village character for years—a man over forty, whose face was nevertheless ageless, with its round cheeks and high forehead unwrinkled and its loose mouth impertinently boyish. His only sober periods were from noon to evening and he had poured a torrent into himself for years, without a break and yet with scarcely a sign of physical deterioration. His life was that of a tramp, or thief on a small scale, and he had passed through untold scores of humiliations, attacks and exposures, yet each night found him with his head once more held high and an air of untouched, self-sufficient drollery. He was a minor Villon who lived entirely for each day and forgot every vestige of it on each successive morning. Dressed in white duck trousers, dirty canvas shoes, gray coat and red shirt, he was grotesque, self-invincible, as he spoke to the other four.

"I'm circulating a radio-pledge—going from door to door and collecting signatures. I'll have thousands of them before the end of the month. Here's the idea."

He drew a piece of typewritten paper from an inside coat-pocket and read: "We, the undersigned, agree not to turn our radio dials to any of the commercially sponsored programs on the air, or listen to them elsewhere, unless they observe the following rules. 1. The hired announcers, dilating on each product, must confine their talks to periods no more than one minute in length, occurring at the very beginning and end of the programs. 2. The announcers must mention the addresses, 'phone numbers and advertised brands of their firms only twice during each talk, instead of twelve or fourteen times, and must act on the presumption that their listeners have some faint vestige of memory. 3. The announcers must not use the same adjectives continually and thus imitate the effect of aspirin tablets. 4. The announcers must not make grotesquely unsubstantiated statements dealing with the sole and unique leadership of their products over those in the same general line. In other words, the announcers must not invariably talk with the conviction that their listeners are, in the aggregate, subnormal, because this is not true. 5. The announcers must not seek to appeal to possible elements of snobbishness in their listeners, with statements alleging that their cigarettes or automobiles are universally used by society people, polo players and devotees of fox-hunting in the winter resorts of North Carolina. 6. The items on the programs must be introduced in a brief, simple fashion and must not be hampered by second-string announcers, recruited from Broadway and filling in time with interminable O.K.'s, stale gags and puns, and tiresome eulogies of the performers. . . . We, the undersigned, pledge ourselves not to listen to the aforementioned abuses, and to ignore the offending programs until they are altered in the interest of common decency and veracity."

After the ripple of laughter had dwindled, a blonde, swollen girl in white canton crêpe asked: "Say, Howie . . . are you going to get the signature of Ring Lardner and his radio column?"

Grannihan exploded.

"Ring Lardner . . . jumping on the titles and the lyrics of the radio song hits and foaming at the mouth . . . calling them smutty, indecent, vile . . . flagrantly immoral . . . a menace to the kiddy-loving American home. Any man who can read smut and indecency into vague, harmless drivel like 'Love Me Tonight,' 'Let's Put Out the Lights and Go to Sleep,' 'Take Me in Your Arms' . . . well, any bird like that is beyond me!"

At another table, several literary celebrities were forgetting their tea-party manners. They had just escaped from one of their profitable but boresome routines, a banquet held in honor of a white lady from China, who had written an enormously best-selling, sentimental, placidly flowery and pathetic version of a Chinese farmer's rise to power and affluence in his locality—a book in the "undangerous" and earthly simple category. The banquet had been the usual array of eulogies, politely felicitous jokes, political amenities and secret piques, and the celebrities now at "George's" were expanding and cutting up in the ache to be human again.

Frank Vinson sat beside Inez, his wife—two members of an assiduous family often laughingly referred to, by writers, as "The Vinson Literary Trust." Vinson was a bulky man with grayish hair and a large, peacefully bear-like face and his wife was a comely, rounded brunette—the acme of shrewd, genial complacency. They danced and jingled with Hubert Clamby and Annabelle Coombs. Annabelle was married to M. M. Billings, another man in the party, and she was little more than a worldly, symmetrical pagan careful enough to hide the gaps in her mental grasp of the seven arts. Clamby had a plastering of red hair and a maliciously boyish face—a man who had published a novel and verse, with neither financial nor critical success, and then turned his attention to the lucrative fad of writing exhaustive biographies partly founded on other biographies of the same person—a fad somewhat less exacting in its demands on imagination. He jostled elbows with Albert and Doris Falkenburg, who were ragging Billings and another woman, Geraldine Tabberson, and being plagued in turn with chaplets of lettuce leaves, tin-foil wreaths. Falkenburg was a man in his late forties, fat-cheeked and goggle-eyed under his spectacles. He affected a bland, chuckling, benign fatherliness on all occasions and scarcely ever confessed an open enmity toward anyone. To rescue the meagre whimsicality of his verses, he had tried other remunerative ventures—a book of sugary, premature memoirs, puppeteering, and the inevitable anthologies. His wife, Doris, was a small, pouting Jewess, thoroughly conventional in her emotions and outlooks, and serving as an excellent foil for Albert's social maneuverings, since her husband neglected few avenues, and one night might find him addressing a Communist defense rally while the next evening discovered him at a Park Avenue soirée.

Billings, on the other hand, carried an air of supercilious boredom varied by condescending smiles—a radical poet—radical in his literary style—who had become the idol and darling of certain erudite, continually squabbling cliques in New York. His friend, Geraldine, was also a poet, more conservative in her verses and possessing a more tactful and gracious character, fully aware of the fact that literary advancement, in New York City, was largely a matter of being friendly to the "right people," disdainful toward the "wrong ones," and creating books not too radical or cutting in their general impact.

At another table a group of Communists—roughly-dressed, loud-voiced men and women—eyed the literary celebrities with a scarcely disguised contempt. The Communists, in turn, received hostile glances from a party of slummers from Washington Heights seated directly behind them. A spirit of actual, general camaraderie did not exist at "George's." It would have been impossible, on a large scale, anywhere in New York—the most predatory, individualistic city on the face of the globe.

Tucked away in a rear corner, Ena Monteith and Romalos sat

with Emil Sperling and a girl named Esther Cohen. Esther was dark and heavy, with straight, black hair falling below her shoulders and the long, severely indented face of an Indian—a girl whose twenty-one years had been stormy, despite the bewildered gentleness of her manner. She had tried to commit suicide by jumping from an uptown bridge spanning the Hudson, but her dress had been caught by the spikes in the railings and she had dangled until she was rescued by passers-by. This episode—headlined and cheaply distorted by the unprincipled tabloid papers of New York City—had induced her parents to send her to a semi-private hospital for the insane. After shamming and uttering the proper, desired statements of repentance, common sense, she had managed to obtain her release from this institution, but her parents still held it as a club over her head, threatening to send her back to the place if she persisted in being rebellious. It was the old story of a non-conformist, a recalcitrant and a dreamer, springing from dictatorial, materialistic, Jewish parents, who could not tolerate the idea that she was utterly different from their own much-prized cautions and repressions—parents who wanted her to dress and act "respectably" and wind up in a marriage with some "wholesome" Jewish business, or professional man.

Esther and Ena were both found of Emil, and Romalos was beginning to resent his seeming exclusion, but the simple jealousy in his black eyes could not decide whether it should laugh at itself or become vehement. He was always afraid of Ena's cutting tongue and yet always longing to oppose it.

"Say, you might give me a tumble once in a while—" His thick lips tried to smile and then abandoned the difficult effort.

Ena regarded him with a challenging compassion.

"Don't be so damn' middle class, Meekie. We're not holding a deliberate contest. Emil isn't competing with you and I'm not flirting with him to lead you on."

"Who said you were? If you're more interested in him . . . fine . . . but I'm entitled to find out about it."

Ena laughed and pinched his cheek.

"You're exactly like the rest of the people here! Look at them. They're all wearing a proprietor's tag pasted on them by *somebody*, and whenever the tag slips, or they're still trying to paste it . . . the old game commences. When they're sober they try to make it a good-natured game and when they drink too much it winds up in a fight, that's all."

The straightness of Ena's words disconcerted Meekie and he scarcely knew whether to be antagonistic, or in agreement. Women weren't supposed to be so blunt, so free from any trace of concealment, teasing sacredness of flesh.

"The way you put it, you make it seem like a joke."

"It is a joke to me, unless it's beautifully candid . . . impulsive . . . accidental. . . ."

Meekie turned the adjectives over in his mind and they were little more than shadowy enemies to his primary feelings, but still he was respectful, distressed against his will. His mind, floundering in a new interpretation of motive and procedure, was barely honest enough to question the more immediate resentments of his heart.

"Aw, to hell with all these accidents. A man wants to have something to hold on to—it's only natural."

Ena's face held a tolerant smile.

"All right then . . . it's a wrestling match to you, and you want to be the winner, but I don't wrestle, except with ideas. If I like you tonight, I'll stay with you, but you'll have to shake up that thick mind of yours first . . . you old, black bumblebee."

Meekie grinned in spite of himself, refreshed by the spirit of hard, smiling challenge which made his own reactions seem slippery, disgruntled nothings to themselves . . . nothings sometimes, and yet aches and angers impossible to kill.

"Well, Ena . . . one of us is a god-damn' fool, but I can never make up my mind which one is the guilty person."

"*Both* of us . . . you fool kid."

Ena leaned forward and kissed his cheek. It was in her nature to melt at the least sign of an unassuming attitude from another person, and to bristle only when the other remained evasive or swaggering.

Emil had listened with the pensive feather of a smile whisking near the corners of his tight mouth. His brown eyes were more peaceful, with less of the old, veiled, humorously dubious bitterness in them. The intervening weeks had changed him somewhat. Under the impact of new people, who seemed to be neither pitying, misunderstanding nor patronizing, he had lost a little of the over-proud, defensive isolation and was not so overcome by the sense of being a physical misfit.

He spoke to Meekie now with a hardness rare for him.

"You're a little too strong for your own good, Meekie. When a man has big muscles he's usually aching to use them on somebody's face, especially when he's got a drink or two under his belt."

Meekie glared, and then his face loosened with an equal swiftness. His first prompting had been the belief that Emil was handing him an insult—under the protection of a crippled condition—but the second thought strove to tell him that this man was only speaking from another world. He stood a bit in awe of Emil's mind, felt that he could not treat the latter with the roughness which was a prerogative among most men. His desire to combat the other's opinions still existed, however, and gave him a forced uneasiness.

"Oh, yeah? Well, I'm not saying anything against brains, but they won't help you much when some big bastard starts to swing at your jaw. Try and use them when a gorilla in a speak' walks up to your girl and squeezes her legs . . . like I've seen."

Esther had been dreaming of a poem which she was planning to write—a poem in which several blind people, with large bells hanging from their chins, backs and knees, were running around in a search for several other people, who were deaf and wearing a medley of colors in the vain attempt to signal to the blind hunters. She awakened just before Meekie's last words.

"Suppose he does squeeze her legs? If he doesn't squeeze too hard and hurt her, I don't see what's wrong about it. And then again, you really ought to ask her whether she liked it or not before you do anything. Some girls are very peculiar. They're always pretending to be angry at somebody else because they're angry at themselves . . . because they liked something when they think they shouldn't have liked it."

Meekie had a pained frown—he could never decide whether Esther was crazy or inspired. She affronted all of his emotions and yet made them helplessly uncertain concerning whether the affront was a legitimate one.

"That's fine. I suppose I ought to write her a note about it and then shake hands with him for touching her up. Honest, you get my goat, Esther."

"Well, if you're in love with each other and she really doesn't want him to touch her, you can both walk away from him, can't you? . . . and then, if he follows you, blow some pepper in his face, quick . . . and you both run out of the place. I know a boy who did that once."

Meekie growled and then said: "You're too much for me, kid. Sometimes you talk just like a baby six years old."

Ena gave Esther a smile of sympathy.

"Keep it up, Es' . . . that he-man audience in the grandstand must get tired of seeing the same old show all the time. It's only their damn' vanity that keeps it going."

"Don't tell me you haven't got any vanity—" Meekie was half joking, half aroused.

"Sure, plenty. That's why I don't always fall into a screaming rage over a physical insult or intrusion. I've never seen a professional fist-swinger yet who wasn't trying to escape from his own, defeated smallness . . . unless he was absolutely forced to defend himself."

Meekie was reflectively silent, lost in an inward turmoil for which he had no instant words. Emil was once more imperturbable.

"The big bastard you were talking about, Meekie . . . he's only a helpless flunky himself. The men who rule this country don't go around smashing faces. They hire other men to do that. They pull the ropes, and hand out the lies, and stir up the hysterias and the enmities. Even among gangsters, the little gorilla goes out and does the dirty work and the leader sits in a night club and acts respectable. If the whole crew of them ever get their faces smashed in, we'll have a new deal, but until then . . . you might as well use your head only and keep your fists tied up."

"Well, I can agree with everything you say, sure . . . but I still want to sock a guy any time he tries to walk over me. I guess the old bean and the muscles just weren't meant to pull together—" Meekie gulped his gin as though he were fortifying himself against all of the futile but, in his opinion, compulsory hatreds in the world.

During the past few weeks Emil had attended Communist

meetings and had become sympathetic toward Communistic doctrines, but he had failed to apply for a membership because he considered the party to be still an impossible joke in this country—an organization run by sentimental humanitarians; shouting, crude gallery-players; self-servers; educated wind-bags completely out of touch with the American proletariat; and prominent, literary converts with large, zealously guarded bank accounts and more easily dispensed indignations. Under such a leadership, he felt that the rank and file of American Communists could only march over the cliff to the inevitable slaughter. The soil was still too barren in America, which would undoubtedly be the last fortress to fall in any worldwide revolution.

As he voiced these mournful impressions to Meekie, Ena interrupted.

"Say, Emil, who's that blonde right opposite us, over against the other wall? She's been staring at us ever since she came in, but I don't know whom she's singling out."

Emil peered through the smoke drifts, past the endless obstructions of bodies, and then, abruptly, recognized Mona.

"Oh, just somebody I know—" Emil lowered his eyes, resisting the strong desire to look again in Mona's direction.

Did he feel ghoulish, digging into the grave of . . . but what grave was ever more than a thick layer of pride, hiding the fitful, the pitifully fitful breathing, which would not quite cease? Negligible things, things capable of destruction, did not need to be buried. Whatever guise they had—thunderstorms or sand grains—it always seemed, afterwards, that they had never occurred, or they became no more than hurried jokes in the dim flirtations of memory. When an emotion needed to be buried, it was never dead. The funeral was a bribe to future stoicism. The mourners were too subtle to be convincing.

Why was he sitting there, asking himself questions, when their embodied answer sat so near him now? The pain of that night in his room with Mona had been more than pain—it had lodged in the fissures of his heart and had become a hated, unfulfilled load, never expelled despite the insistence of his other emotions that it failed to exist. After assuring himself that he detested her, that she was ordinary, conceited, obtuse, he had become slowly unnerved by the fact that he could not dismiss her. The unerring touch of her body, the heart-scent spilling from her face, and all of the urgencies of giving, far beyond humbleness and pride—he could not bring himself to believe that she had simulated them. The disbelief was a lingering intuition and not a mere youthful throe of vanity. In her love-making she had recognized him as a physical equal, had thrown herself to the clutch of his heart and mind, and then another side had rushed forth—streetwise, scoffing, mangling—to make her once more spitefully superior to herself.

Still, youth often reviles its deepest instincts, kicks its own longings in the face. When Mona had approached him at his newsstand, several times after that night, he had repulsed her with short, barely polite words, intent upon avenging his pride. Then, when he was on the edge of relenting, she disappeared and he discovered that she had lost her job after a quarrel with the amorous Tressina. He berated her now, repeated that she was paltry, far below Ena and Esther, but the berating disappeared within the very next sigh from his tight mouth. Emotions were not concerned with plausible matters. Call the wine cheap, but still it flooded, disrupted, every crevice of his heart and mind. Mona was intelligence and denseness, honesty and deceit, delicacy and crudeness—earth personified ... and she was exceptional only in the fact that she had glimpses of what she was, that she struggled against herself with the ever-unexplained restlessness, which separated the groper from the clod.

These feelings—tantalized by the foregoing words rather than shaping them—visited Emil as he stared back at Mona through the shifting people, the hazy air, of the "Rendezvous." Mona smiled steadily at him—a smile which seemed to be inextricably apologetic, flippant, even mournful, and before he realized it he was returning the smile, waving a hand in greeting.

Mona was sitting beside Tommy Burger, her escort of the night. She had been drinking but she was fully in control of herself. She wore a dark-red evening gown with a gardenia pinned on one side, just above the high swelling of her breasts. Under the scanty touch of cosmetics, her broad face seemed to be almost as perilously, transiently white as the gardenia. The green eyes were sad—a sadness disrespectful toward its own tenure—and she was continually fiddling with the cascade of golden hair on her head, not from the usual nervous primping, but because the sight of Emil had ruined her poise. This was her second night with Burger. She had been casually acquainted with him before, through Alicia, and had met him again at a Harlem cabaret, a week before. She regarded him as an average, limited man—a man with the familiar, flip-tongued, unconsciously cruel, hurried essence of New York oozing from every pore of his body. Sometimes he was roughly, or smoothly, entertaining, but more often only endurable. He purred when he was agreed with or admired. He became cold, or sullen, when he encountered opposition, denial. He had a reliable string of jokes, bits of worldly knowledge. In the company of women, he spent money freely for "a good time," drinks, to make the women realize his importance and because he hoped that the alcohol would cause them to become more compliant. When he was sober, he held himself fairly in restraint, and when he was drunk he became nastily domineering. Sexually, he had a trimly cut, plainly muscular appeal, and Mona could have taken him, on a gin-loosened night, and dismissed him on the very next morning—a little disgusted with herself and desiring never to see him again.

She had evaded his advances for a double reason. Having heard the story of his collision with Rosenbaum and Alicia, she was particularly anxious not to give him an opportunity to exercise his authority at her own expense. It was really necessary for some men to discover that every woman was not precisely *glued* to the knuckles on their fists. Again, she had denied her body to all men since the night with Emil and Bingham because she had continued to hate herself—below the hundreds of laughters, defenses, attempted distractions—and men had become, compulsorily, the indirect targets of this mood.

When Emil finally answered her smile, she was happy and defiling her happiness, in one breath. Her heart threw off the slang boredom, the over-worked, feminine inflations, and then ... So, the little tin Jesus had consented to notice her, after sneaking glances at her for the past half hour and only after she had lowered herself by smiling first, like a numbskull brat begging to be forgiven. To be forgiven ... for what? Her conscience muttered in a slow dripping, of blood drops near the sound of sophistical words, all the convenient, sanguine words which meant nothing to the swiftness of emotion. It was a torture for her to admit that she might be a fool—a brassily talkative, fidgeting, untalented woman, who had walked out of a crippled boy's room one night, furious and wretched at one and the same time because her own sense of snug, half-blind vigor, otherwise known as normality, had been overwhelmed but not destroyed. Why did she turn hot and cold, lose her confidence, feel cheap to herself, whenever she ran across that kid?

He wasn't a compelling male, according to any of her previous definitions, and yet he made these definitions sick of their own continuity. He was "crazy," gentle, "arty," hard to grasp, but in her remembrance of him he was almost unbearably nude, speaking and acting in straight lines, shy and then, suddenly, the wedding-march between softness and harshness when he was faced by persistent evasion from another person, when he was forced to hate his own momentary desire to evade, to become what people designated as "socially poised." Groping toward these impressions, she told herself that Emil was a nut and a baby, and he would have been *some* hell-raiser, if life had not twisted his body, and he was a softy and yet couldn't be easily squashed. Hitherto, she had bowed to the Ernest Hemingway idea—the ever-active, magnified he-man, with just enough mentality to lend an appearance of variety and introspection to his brutal fatalisms, and with moments of rough tenderness, choked repentance, to make the dominant animal within him more enticing—the figure worshipped by shop-girls and feminine book reviewers alike. Emil was at the opposite extreme to Mona, and yet he was bringing her, inch by inch, to the belief that delicateness was not necessarily repugnant, or inappropriate, in a man, and that a man might possess it to a high degree and still remain definitely masculine.

Tearing her eyes from Emil, she spoke to Burger.

"Carry me out on a stretcher, Tommy."

"Yeah? What for? You've had exactly two drinks so far, and I haven't punched you . . . yet."

"Do me a favor, will you?"

"Sure, what is it?"

"Punch yourself . . . hard."

He looked at her with a smooth unconcern on his close mouth, which was always rigid when he was not talking and, otherwise, seemed to move reluctantly. Insults from women were tolerated in his code and dismissed as sharp kiddings in the little sham battle between a man and a woman, unless they were persistent or sexual jabs. His voice was casual.

"Don't get rough—I might bite you."

"That would be a social error, Mr. Burger."

"Are you fond of etiquette, Miss Farrideau?"

"Sometimes... especially from men who are too conceited, Mr. Burger."

"Does that refer to me, Miss Farrideau?"

"Why, of course not. You're so bashful and retiring, Mr. Burger. It *couldn't* be you."

He laughed, briefly, to hide a first irritation, since the last sarcasm had been too blunt for his vanity to swallow.

"The party's getting too friendly. Let's have another drink and see if we can't be enemies."

"You *are* an optimist, but I need the drink, so it doesn't matter."

His face was coldly planning as he leaned forward to retrieve the bottle of Scotch, which stood under the table. He regarded Mona as a desirable but opinionated and over-indulged woman; and he could have kissed and slapped her, in rotation and without undue compunction because she galled and yet invited his masculine exaggerations. He intended to flirt with one of the girls at the table to his left—a girl who had been trading side-glances with him. Apart from any plain desire to make Mona jealous, he wanted to give an experimental uncertainty to his night and remain the chooser, the string-puller. He was always the great male—the individual who scarcely ever deserted the swaggers, the grim, or jovially placid, sufficiencies without which the entire delusion of his ego would have fallen to bits.

The girl to his left was obviously unattached and sitting with a man and another girl, who were exchanging endearments and including her, rather patronizingly, in their sporadic conversation. She wore an old rose and egg-shell ensemble and she had the face of a rounded, piquant infant beneath fluffs of chestnut hair. Mona noticed the hovering of guarded smiles between Burger and the other girl, and she was sneeringly relieved. The Great God Burger was about to admit another subject into his realm. Now she had a pretext for escaping—a few minutes of respite. Rising, she said: "I'm going to talk to a friend of mine. I'm sure you'll make good use of the time while I'm away."

"Cheerio and God bless you—" Burger affected a cross between nonchalance and arrogance.

Emil greeted Mona with a timid delight and made one of the waitresses bring a chair for her. The first, tentative amenities petered out and then the drama intruded, swiftly. Emil and Mona became inevitably constrained. They were over-brimming and yet silent with words and emotions which required a more private setting. They faltered subtly between the mutilations of pride and the deeper desire to understand each other. The enormous attraction between them was handicapped, in its immediate expression, because it was still forced to hack its way through the different worlds in which they lived when they were not face to face. Again, they had started with a misadventure and this can often create a rankling rhythm leading to other errors, other strangulations, before it is finally overcome by the even stronger desire, which slowly fights against it. Among sensitive people, accident often attends the birth of their emotions, as an efficient or bungling midwife, despite the facile desire of novelists to give their characters an orderly and independent development.

Mona was upset as she talked to Emil now—trepidant, flighty and inarticulate. In Emil the warfare was more clearly drawn—instinct and emotion on one side, mind and spirit on the other, with deserting tremors from both lines continually making the conflict inconclusive. In his youthful fashion he tried to be judicious, sophisticated, even joking, as he spoke, but he failed because the effort itself failed to interest him. Hell, all of this talking, *talking* ... the clatter and jumble of it rang in his ears now, from hundreds of surrounding voices in "George's," and when it was all over, emotion still remained unconsumed, tormented, stubborn.

Esther was indifferent to Mona, since Esther liked only those few women who were basic children and went on wild splurges of imagination, while Romalos thought that Mona was a fast-stepping broad, having a good time by mixing with people whom she probably regarded as a bunch of nuts.

"Why don't you bring your friend over to meet us?" Emil smiled, uncertainly.

"Bring *him*? Why, say ... his face would be a beautiful magenta if he sat here five minutes, and it wouldn't be embarrassment either—" Mona glanced in the direction of Burger, with half-hearted derision.

"Do you like him?"

"No ... not particularly."

"Then why do you go out with him?"

Mona felt blue, disconcerted, dispersed.

"Are you putting me on the witness stand?"

"I'm not a lawyer. Maybe I'm just an overgrown child with a little curiosity."

"Well, if I only went out with the men I liked, I'd be a hermit most of the time."

"Do you like me, Mona?"

"Say... are you a question bag?"

"No, I'm just talking because I don't know what to say. Perhaps I ought to be silent."

Mona was in a flurry of irritation and wistfulness.

"You're a strange kid, Emil. I like you but well, you rattle me, I guess."

"I wish I didn't."

"Oh, it isn't your fault. I've acted like an idiot to you, and I don't know how to atone for it."

"It wasn't idiocy. You stepped out of your own world and out of your own feelings, for a time, and then you came to your senses and you were angry at yourself. I understand."

If he had assailed her, Mona would have been combative and yet relieved, but his words seemed patronizing now and she hated them.

"Is there anything you *don't* understand? Honest, you're just a little too wise to be true."

Emil felt that he had been slapped without reason by a woman who was mysteriously determined to hide from both herself and him, and he tried to become coldly armored now.

"Have it your own way. I don't understand you, and you've made up your mind not to give me the slightest help. I'm beginning to wonder why you came over to talk to me."

The silence was inept, tired of its own impediments. Ena Monteith had been listening with an impatient contempt on her straight, wild face. The impending fray between Ena and Mona was inevitable. They were not without emotional resemblances—the tendency to exaggerate in one breath and apologize in the next—and they shared a high-strung longing to be naked in mind and heart, but their lives had been too different. Mona had been taught to hug thousands of verbal veils from which Ena had escaped. Ena spoke to Mona in a hard, quick voice:

"Oh, you . . . you make me tired. Everything you say is just another side-step. I know what happened between you and Emil that night you were in his room. You were overwhelmed by his mind, his imagination. He was the kind of a man you hadn't met before, and you wanted to bring a gift to his loneliness—something less elusive than words. *That* part of it was clear and spontaneous, but afterwards, you were too small to understand your own feelings. You acted like you had thrown a scrap to a poor, little doggie because you wanted to feel safe, and ordinary, and important again. You're exactly like a hundred other women I know."

The intrusion, with its utter lack of reticence, niceties, and, in her opinion, insight, infuriated Mona. She was convinced that Ena had attempted to disrobe her, with a vulgar cruelty, because Ena wanted to pose as a marvel of candor and emancipation, and thus elevate herself in the estimation of Emil.

"I must say . . . I admire your nerve. You've hardly met me, you don't know a thing about me, and yet you're telling the world exactly what I am. . . . I suppose I'm middle class to you because I don't act like a freak and throw everything to the winds, and I'm not straining all the time, trying to show people how wonderfully free and superior I am. That's really too bad, isn't it?"

Ena was unruffled now and her voice was slow, almost softened.

"I don't know what's good or bad. I just spoke out what happened to be on my mind—that's an occasional habit of mine."

"It's a charming habit, really. I think all of you ought to walk around with sandwich boards, advertising everybody's intimate affairs."

Ena was smiling and unconcerned. She had no conscious, personal bias toward Mona and, to herself, she had only voiced her general code of conduct, in which concealments of any kind were unnecessary and intolerable.

"I'm not an advertising agent and I'm not trying to be superior. I don't like to play any kind of a social game and most people do, but if I had to choose, I'd much rather wear a sandwich board than spend all my time putting on different dresses and composing my face. I don't like monotones of any kind. Maybe that's why you think I'm a freak."

"Never mind that—I called you a freak because I had every right to be sore. Evidently you go around treating everybody in a slam-bang fashion, but I won't stand for it. You keep your nose out of my business... please. You didn't take the trouble to talk to me first and try and understand me. Oh, no. You wanted to put me on the pan just because you know I'm different from what you are, that's all."

No longer confidently angry, Mona had become inquisitive and distressed underneath her words. Ena was an obnoxious mystery to Mona and she could not decide whether Ena was a glib trickster or a more honest figure never before duplicated in her previous experience.

Emil was confused and perturbed, feeling infinitely like a five-year-old, sulking and miserably tongue-tied while his elders staged a contention, which made him self-conscious and, somehow, ridiculous to himself. He dreaded his present position wherein, to outsiders, he might seem to be the complacent male enjoying the feminine wrangle which he had caused. He was also torn between loyalties. Ena was the ingratiating barbarian, who had swept him out of his loneliness, introduced him to interesting people, treated him with a gaiety verging on the impersonal, but now he resented her remarks, her endless disregard for privacy and restraint of any kind. He felt that Mona was a struggler—a girl fighting against her past environments and her own envies, shrinkings—and his heart reached out to her.

"I wish we could all be . . . peaceful. It would be such a novelty. I'm tired of all this misunderstanding . . . and I'm tired of always taking myself and my ideas seriously—" Emil looked at Mona and Ena with a wistfulness near to humility.

The drama trailed off to an anti-climax. Mona tried to say something gracious, faltered, and then, tossing her head, abruptly left the table. Ena—sullen and removed now—departed with Romalos. Esther snuggled against Emil and told him that he should not continue to be hurt because pain was only a beggar wandering forever through a crowd of people, who imagined that they were rich, and when the people became beggars themselves, pain was forced to slink away because, then, he lost his reason for existence. The heaviness in Emil's heart smiled in spite of itself. Esther lived in her own world—a world in which everything was translated in fable, imagery and the most infinitely delicate simplicity—and this realm was far apart from the direct, realistic contentions and maneuvers which engrossed other people. Esther's world could be regarded as a mass of flimsy conceits, of idly distorted whimsies and escapes, and yet . . . it was sometimes a necessary and appealing antidote against all of the heavier self-importances in life—the great sexual, economic, scientific and philosophical promisers and bogiemen. They solved nothing and extracted too much from heart and mind, and they needed to be ignored and chastened, occasionally.

Emil was far from being in love with Esther, but she made all of the youth in his veins feel like a protective father in the presence of a helpless, fantastic child. He joined her playful images now and tried to forget that Mona, the woman who affronted and tantalized him in one and the same breath, was still seated near him, still quickening his heart-beats.

Returning to Burger, Mona found him embracing the girl in the old rose and egg-shell ensemble and kissing her with a drunken gusto, while she squirmed and responded, alternately, in the manner of a woman whose inhibitions were still fighting against the careless, silly feeling, the hazy promiscuity, which alcohol brings to certain people. Women of her kind could be natural only when they were tipsy, and always discovered, on the next morning, that they needed to be once more respectable and repentant. Burger looked up at Mona with an appraising insolence.

"Don't mind me, lady. You go right out and have a good time yourself, until we leave this joint here. Go right ahead."

Mona's pride, scarcely recovered from the previous barrage, showed its teeth now.

"Do you know, there must be some reason for your existence, Tommy, but I've never been able to figure it out."

Immediately after she had uttered the words, she turned and walked away, intending to secure her coat from the cloak-room in the rear and leave the place. As she was about to cross the dance floor she felt a hand on her arm, and halted. Stanley Bingham was standing beside her. His tuxedo outfit was immaculate, even to the white carnation pinned in his lapel, and standing there, tall and conventionally handsome, he seemed once more a welcome refuge, a safe and "wholesome" medium between the virulence of a Burger and the shy and yet taunting involvements of Emil Sperling. The smile on his face was forced and he appeared to be disgusted with the night in general.

"Hello, babe."

"Hello, Stan."

After a moment of silence, Mona spoke again.

"We certainly seem to run across each other at the most unearthly times."

"Blue times would suit me better."

"Why, what's the trouble, Stan?"

His straight-nosed face had a blunt weariness.

"Oh, everything and nothing. Did you ever notice how boresome people are when they're drinking and you're sober?"

"Did I?—I'll say. Why, sometimes I think they all drink because that's the only way they can become really interested in each other, but . . . we're not much better, Stan."

"No, I suppose not—" He sighed and fidgeted with his tie, and then he asked: "Say, why did you run away from me that night?"

"Oh, I was seeing things because I'd hurt another man just before I met you, but . . . well . . . it doesn't matter. Forget about it. Are you alone tonight?"

Bingham grinned coldly.

"Yes and no. I started out with a girl, but after she'd had several drinks she decided the fat gentleman at the next table was more appealing. She's sitting over there against the wall—the one in the green dress."

He waved his hand toward a blossomy, squealing chunk of a girl who was rubbing cheeks with a corpulent, horsey man near his forties. Mona laughed—a short, vicious sound.

"I'm in exactly the same boat, only I can't stand the man who took me out, so I'm going to leave him with his new conquest."

"Are you listenin', radio-folks? It is now one forty-five—full-of-bull watch-time. What do you say? Suppose we amble into the deep and mysterious night?"

"Amscray?"

"Rightscray."

While Bingham was paying the check at the door and explaining the transference, she turned for a last stare at Emil. He was conversing with Esther about the personified daisies on the moon—daisies a mile wide, with zigzagging stems, mauve petals and sun-clear pollens—and he did not see Mona standing in the doorway. He had resigned himself to defeat, on this night at least, and had buried her once more as an impossible ache and tremor waiting for resurrection in the dark patience of his heart. Within Mona, scorn and dismay were exactly matched. The little, funny, sweet, conceited, god-damn', beautiful, weak, baffling tin Jesus. Let him stay with his deep girls, with their high-brow twists of gab, who were always hanging their clothes out to dry. Nevertheless, a quiver remained and bided its time—the realization that this soft-voiced, crippled boy had a mind and a heart able to goad her into every variation of begging smallness, despite her disclaimers and beyond any mere alliance of sentimentality and pity.

She accepted Bingham's invitation to visit his apartment on Riverside Drive near One Hundred and Sixteenth Street, and as they rode up in his black sedan, she leaned against one of his arms, as he directed the wheel, and tried to tell herself that he was the man whom she needed—a good, hearty norm, neither petty nor noble, who would take care of her, throw a blanket over her troubles and doubts, and rescue her from the old, alarm-clock farce. When they almost collided with a taxi and he was forced to swerve sharply over the curb, she was only a bit excited and amused, and she thought about it afterwards. People were only afraid to die when they were happy or sad but still a little hopeful. Otherwise, they might not commit suicide, but their interest in life was only a habit, a dramatic sham.

The machine shot up Riverside Drive past the Soldiers' and Sailors' Memorial—slabs of gray stone, with stone effigies of human beings standing, kneeling and posturing, like frozen slaves, without life or death, and unaware of the essentially fraudulent reverence and sorrowful respect, which they were supposed to symbolize. The dying green, steep slopes of Riverside Park, sprinkled with trees, bushes, and cement walks, looked down upon the river-front, which was an expanse of hillocky earth, weeds, tin cans, railroad tracks. The contrast was New York City incarnate, where pretentious order and slovenly disorder shouldered one another in the innate dilemma which is prose.

Bingham's three-room apartment was furnished with an average definition of good taste—solid, dark oak tables and chairs, gray and green Axminster rugs, a grand piano, old English prints and subdued hangings. As Bingham stood before the side-board, mixing a shaker of cocktails, he turned sometimes and looked at Mona with a desire which was respectfully hesitant, nervous. She was reclining on a broad divan, with one hand over her eyes, and, in spite of her stoutness, a certain, firmly delicate, trim fusion of lines made her seem to be much less substantial. Suddenly, Bingham grew vastly sentimental. In his estimation, Mona's mind was amazingly practical and yet profound—for a woman—and he felt that he was tired of all the good-looking nitwits who chattered about nothing or were just wise enough to remain silent most of the time and thus escape from betraying themselves.

He thought that Mona was undoubtedly an ideal compromise. He shrank from "excessively cultured" or professional women, because they made him feel inadequate beneath his refusal to admit this reaction, and Mona, to him, represented a more natural woman—one with her feet planted on the earth, who could nevertheless rise to an appreciation of the deeper and more beautiful things in life, occasionally. A man could take her to the opera or to a good lecture without being ashamed of any comments which she might make, and then whirl her away to a midnight of jazz and fun. He had been thinking of her continually since the insult, the abrupt desertion, which she had inflicted on him, and after regarding her as a pugnacious enigma he had finally decided that her conduct had been caused by a drunken mania unattached to her real character. Alcohol played queer tricks on human beings; he himself had once fractured the jaw of his best pal and risen on the next morning without the slightest remembrance of it.

Only his stubbornly injured vanity had kept him from writing or telephoning Mona during the intervening weeks—that vanity which reveals the innately helpless condition of thought existing in most human beings.... Sipping cocktails with Mona now, on the divan, Stanley sought to be poetic.

"You know, living in New York all the time, a person doesn't appreciate the simple things in life, like ... well ... like watching a sunset ... or admiring flowers ... or going on a long hike down a country road."

Mona's broad, milkish-cream face was sleepily removed.

"Have you tried the stuff they call Nervine? I've heard it's a wonderful tonic, Stan."

"Say, are you going to be like all the rest of them—just a good time and a hey-nonny-nonny?"

"I wish it were a good time. We're only kidding ourselves. Go into thousands of places every night and it's always the same story.

They drink because they're not really happy."

"Then you think a happy person doesn't need to drink."

"I think nothing of the kind. I said most people in New York drink because they're not really happy. You can tell a happy drinker every time. The more he drinks the quieter he becomes. He imagines he's Buddha then, I suppose."

Bingham had risen and was strolling nervously.

"I don't know what we're coming to. This is a crazy age all right. We live too fast and we work too hard, and there's no real friendship in the air."

Mona stretched her legs out on the divan and looked compassionate. Here was a man like herself, without much talent, groping for something different, something more lovely and stirring than the routines of work, night life.

"You're not a bad kid, Stan."

He sat beside her, held her hand. He looked at her full bosom and the elastic sweep of her legs, but it was not simply lust. He had become a pagan sentimentalized to a degree where sex was treated gingerly, in the desperate attempt to imagine that it was new, incredibly rapturous.

"The same goes for you, Mona. I could take breakfast with you for the rest of my life, I guess."

"You must keep a straight face, whatever you do."

"But I mean it. I'll marry you in a second, if you'll have me."

"Is this a serious proposal?"

"Nothing else. They're always warbling about it on Tin Pan Alley. I think it's called love."

"But I'm not in love with you. I like you very much. Wait awhile and let's see what happens."

"You'll give me a chance anyway."

"All the chance in the world, Stan."

He kissed her cheeks, fondled her throat and shoulders and felt revived and gallant, to himself, despite his disappointed vanity. Running her fingers through his hair, she grew miserable again. What was the answer to the riddle—so many human beings chasing something which they couldn't capture and slapping it, refusing to recognize it, when they did capture it? It was sometimes like a merry-go-round of motives, dizzy and invisible. She wanted a crippled kid with a funny, amazing bean, and clear, straight eyes, and a way of making her uncomfortable, blue, eager . . . what was it all about? Stanley wanted her and he was a warm, pleasant compromise. Oh, the devil with this whole-loaf-or-nothing stuff!

"You can have me, Stan—" Mona whispered the words as Bingham leaned over to kiss her shoulders.

In spite of his desire, he was reluctant to leave the "niceness" of the situation. He had refined his feelings to a wistful condition bordering on timidity—a rare departure in which the he-man acknowledged that he was bored with his muscles, his practical swaggers, his pursuit of money.

"Are you sure you want to?"

"Not unless you are."

Suddenly, he felt tired of words, felt that people spoke them largely to escape from seeing themselves too clearly. It was a moment of intuition usually foreign to his heavy and limited nature—the mystery which psychologists pretend to be able to classify under the phrase "sublimated release." Still gentle, he kissed her breasts, stroked her body, and became strange and loftily whirling, to himself. Taking his mouth, gripping his shoulders, Mona was embarrassed, compelled to admit that, in spite of the present sweetness, narcotic, disrobing, she was still thinking of Emil Sperling, still pledging herself to him beyond this immediate lyricism of nerves.

II

Alicia emerged from the One Hundred and Eighty-first Street subway station .and walked up the street leading to Broadway. She was going to pay a surprise visit to Rosenbaum's apartment, since she had not seen him for two days and had heard, from one of the bartenders at his speakeasy, that he was ill. The time was nearing 2 A.M. and few people were on the streets. The apartment buildings, five and six stories high, were all without individuality and yet trying to emulate it with little, minor differences—ornamental, stone fountain-basins; brass-rimmed door-lights with a slightly Londonish touch; fluted cornices; cherub-faces of stone over the entrances; uneven courtyards and scrolls on the roof corners. All of them sported fancy names—the Eulalie, Morningside Manor, the Riverview, the Princess Marjorie. It was an amusing New York touch—undistinguished prose forever trying to forget itself by writing its signatures with a scroll and a flourish.

On the near-by river, boats honked and wailed. Close at hand, taxis whizzed down the pavements and shot around corners—a menace to the unwary pedestrian. The last of the jazz bands blared from radios and could be heard faintly on the street. In a doorway, a man and a woman were earnestly slapping each other's faces. In another hallway one could glimpse a boy and a girl forced to embrace furtively, with glances continually directed toward the entrance. The few passers-by walked swiftly, looking at one another out of the corners of their eyes. Even in this section, far uptown, the tension and distrust, which was one part of New York, still manifested itself.

NEW YORK MADNESS

Alicia was in one of her rarely joyous moods. They never seemed to spring from any tangible reason or event, and it was as though another, spooky self within her came and went, without warning. She was wearing a sky-blue beret, from which the rivulets of her black hair streamed, and her elastic mouth held the embryo of a smile. She did not dare to smile more openly because a woman, alone and smiling, issued an obvious invitation in the opinion of certain males. The attitudes were widespread in New York City, where unacquainted people—unless they were drunk or well on the road to it—treated one another in a cautious, unnatural, mundane fashion in public places.

Sheering into the court-yard of an apartment house on Morningside Avenue, Alicia proceeded to Rosenbaum's flat. The Negro elevator boy and switchboard attendant looked, grinned covertly, and said nothing—liberal tips came to him who minded his own business in little old New York. Alicia pressed the outside buzzer beside Rosenbaum's door. He opened the door and stood there, dressed in a dark-blue lounging-robe, gray trousers and black slippers. His sallow, thin-lipped face was chagrined, repentant, muddled.

"Hello, babykins. Come in."

She sensed that he was not alone.

"I heard you were sick so I thought I'd run up and play nurse to you, but . . ."

"But what?"

"You've got another one with you now . . . I know."

"Yes, but that doesn't matter."

"Oh, doesn't it though?"

"No. You're coming in if I have to drag you."

After he had half pulled her through the doorway, their eyes examined each other. Still partly in the rhythm of a joyous mood Alicia found it difficult to take her own jealousy seriously, to gain the intensely frustrated blindness of anger, but she did feel a sinking, a beckoning to fear, which began to steal over the previous gaiety. Joe was troubled, trying to be unconcerned and despite his surface sophistication, like a boy who had been caught in a crime, as he placed her coat and beret on the hanger. Undoubtedly, sex was the labyrinth between animal nudeness and ethereal music, a labyrinth in which any degree of careless or wistful honesty seemed to be almost impossible. He blamed himself now, shrank from his own actions, in spite of the fact that blame was scarcely more than a joke. He had been tempted to make another woman happy—a woman humbly and insanely in love with him—but not merely from a flattered ego, from the balmy delusions of kindness. The matter had been more subtle than that. He actually liked the other woman enough to miss completeness by a scant breath, sometimes, and at other times it was gratitude and desperation too involved to exist as a coherent motive. Alicia was caprice and abandon, welcome and refusal—the perilous tumult of earth. Anna Stephens was attainable and Alicia essentially unattainable, no matter how often he seemed to possess her.

They were standing in the first living-room now—Alicia, Joe and Anna. The slopes of Anna's bosom and hips were reminiscent of hills clear against some sky—sturdy, effortlessly competent. She had bright red hair, hastily pinned to a rolling effect just below the nape of her neck, and her face was a bit lopsidedly round, with a suspicion of freckles and bluish-gray eyes—incidents of storm and clearing together—and a boyishly heavy mouth. She was wearing a loose, pink chemise and black pumps, and it was obvious that she had been interrupted in the process of hastily dressing herself. Alicia strolled to the walnut table in the center of the room and fingered one of the books lying upon it, as she inclined her head and waited for Joe to make the introduction. When this formality had been completed—the meaningless monosyllables—Anna glanced down at her chemise, ever so quickly, ruefully, and said: "Oh, will you excuse me, please? I might as well finish dressing—I'll be more comfortable."

"Certainly, go ahead—" Alicia thought that she was displaying an excellent sportsmanship.

Joe remained silent, pretending to be immersed in the selection and lighting of a cigarette, and he was inwardly agitated despite the self-amusement which lurked in the agitation. If he had been a gentleman, he would not have allowed Alicia to enter the apartment, but then, being a gentleman was always contradictory to any man's impulse, especially his initial impulse. The woman whom he loved and the one he respected, but only with an errant tenderness—he thought that the conflict was unequal and yet fair. After all, Alicia had faced something of the same prospect on that night when he had fought with Burger. Anna, the object of his respect, his flitting contentment in her arms—was it only that? Emotions could always be surprising in their unexpected deaths and resurrections, and it was ridiculous to be absolutely certain of any phase of the heart.

Alicia averted her head from Joe, who stood on the other side of the table and looked at her with love and self-reproach convulsive on his face. He could not think of a single word to say that would not have been a half-witted intrusion into a situation where actions were much more incipient than words. Alicia's emotions rose and fell in the swiftest of contentions. Her pride writhed and laughed at itself. Her vanity jeered and snivelled by turns. She was angry at herself for having caused Joe's derelictions, and angry at him because he had accepted the challenge instead of bowing to it—knowing that, if he had bowed, she would have despised him. She had all of the fluctuations of a woman who had played with the man whom she loved—to enjoy an independence never quite real to itself—and who was now shrinking from, and attacking, the inevitable results. Anna emerged from the bedroom, with a white silk blouse tucked into a black skirt, and her hair pinned in neat coils at the back of her head. Alicia and Joe were circling between the table and a corner-desk—still avoiding each other's faces. Anna spoke immediately.

"I want him to be happy—that's my only consideration. I'm tired of this conniving. Things will have to be decided tonight, once and forever."

The bluntness, quietly voiced, flustered Alicia. She was irritated and yet admiring.

"I don't want to take part in any contest for Joe. He can do as he pleases. I wouldn't have come in here if he hadn't pulled me through the doorway."

Anna stood in front of Alicia now.

"You have a great deal of pride, haven't you?"

"Yes, I think so."

"Well, so have I, but let's not cover up this time. You're always quarreling with Joe and yet you can't stay away from him. Why in God's name don't you go and live with him, or give him up? If you'll really stick with him, I'll step aside . . . no matter how much it hurts me."

Joe hovered around the desk in the corner, and he felt morose and cheap. He had no desire to parade as the smug male, puffed up because two women were contending for him, and yet he thought that such a semblance was being forced upon him. He wanted to cling to Alicia without injuring Anna—an impossibility—and he could see no escape from the vise.

Anna's last words had angered Alicia.

"Oh, stop pulling this angel idea. You'll step aside! You'll do nothing of the kind. You're as unscrupulous as any other woman is when she's in love, but you want to appeal to his sympathies and show him how noble you are."

As she sat on the arm of a chair, close to Alicia, Anna's heavy mouth was sad without malice. Innately a sentimentalist, she was nevertheless capable of refining it to a relatively impersonal retreat. She found herself unable to dislike Alicia because she told herself that she understood the other woman too well. To her, Alicia held all of the preponderances so inherently a part of the feminine sex—the willful concealments; the erratic flights between tenderness and self-protection; the spiteful dodges and coercions; the perpetual groping toward an ideal substance, which changed so often to a mere will-o'-the-wisp the moment it was touched. Anna's love for Joe was a deep exaltation and abasement combined. He was the only man whom she had ever recognized as superior to herself. She considered him to be a poet stilled by an unfortunate life, a dreamer compelled to mingle with practical animals and somehow hold them at arm's length, and a man whose weaknesses were human and understandable—fits of indolence and sneering apathy, and unconscious cruelties directed equally against himself and other people. In addition, he gave her the unbalanced, breath-stopping, fire-veined effacement, which is the height of physical and yet unphysical love, and which psychologists can never quite explain or analyze.

The silence was like a weighty pendulum, as the three shifted around the room. When Anna spoke, she was barely audible.

"Oh, I'm so sick of all this misunderstanding. I'm not trying to pose as a virtuous person. I know he's in love with you and I'm willing to give him up, if you'll do your part, but if you're going to keep up all this fighting and disappearing and coming back again ... well ... then I feel that I've got the right to compensate him for your neglect, and I won't allow anything to stop me either."

Alicia was calmer now. Somehow, Alicia found herself liking this clear-speaking woman, against all of the lingerings of suspicion and rancor. She walked up to Anna and dropped a hand on her shoulder.

"You're much better for Joe than I am. He needs a mother and a nurse and a secretary, that boy, and I'm afraid I can't fill the bill, so I suppose I ought to walk out of the picture."

Anna patted Alicia's hand for a moment.

"If anybody walks out, it's going to be me. I've known all the time I didn't have a chance, but I've been hanging on because I thought both of you would split up permanently some day, and then I could be ... well ... the consolation prize, I suppose ... but it never happens that way."

Touched, uprooted a bit from herself, Alicia returned the caress.

"I think we'd both be better off if we left him alone and started all over again."

The situation had become unendurable to Joe. He felt ridiculous, puppet-like, unfairly described. He approached the women and stood frowning at them.

"Listen, I haven't clapped any hand-cuffs on either one of you. If you really think I'm ruining your lives, you can walk off and forget about me."

"Joe, don't be melodramatic—" Alicia's voice was grudgingly tender.

"I'm not, but my feelings seem to be the last thing to be considered. I've tried to be reasonably honest with both of you. I told Anna I didn't love her—in the deeper meaning of the word—and what I've told *you* would fill a book."

"I'm not attacking you, Joe."

"No, but that queenly air of yours is irritating, to say the least. I'm not a schoolboy and you're not a couple of mothers deciding whether I ought to be whipped."

The silence became suddenly dejected. Anna approached Joe and stroked his cheeks before she spoke.

"You are a schoolboy, but you've got to pretend to be hard and sophisticated. Only rats and fools and peacocks are really sophisticated, Joe. They're willing to sell their feeble imaginations for a guaranteed set of smooth manners and rules."

"If I sold my imagination, I'd get a remarkably low price."

"Yes, from most people. You were born to be an artist, but you couldn't believe in yourself."

"Oh, well, I think we're all basically insignificant, for that matter. It's all an incredible mixture of happiness and sadness, outside of the arts and sciences, and I may be just as important and . . . just as little important in the sum total of time as any artist or scientist. I like to say that anyway."

Spontaneously, he and Anna kissed each other, and his hands pressed into the sides of her breasts and her waist for seconds. Why couldn't he love this woman, with her alert, straight mind and her sweet, sturdy body? She was really "too damn' good for him"—that was probably the trouble. As Anna touched Joe, she shivered and glimpsed the shaping of a finale which neither of them desired, or were able to evade.

Alicia had been strolling around the room, depressed and feeling mentally inferior to Anna against her own admission. She halted beside Joe.

"Joe, can I talk to you alone for a minute?"

She turned to Anna.

"Please don't mind. I'm not trying to put over anything sly, really I'm not, but I'd be embarrassed if you heard what I want to tell him."

"Of course ... I understand—" Anna smiled feebly.

She was tightening herself to a renunciation which taxed every inch of her resources, and for seconds the room spun in front of her eyes, while Joe became a ghost pleading for life and Alicia was scarcely more than a funeral director seeking desperately to be honest in the midst of her inevitable jealousies.

Joe and Alicia retired to a rear bedroom and faced each other. Alicia was despondent, almost tearful.

"Do you want me to give you up, Joe? Tell me."

He stared at her—indecisive, feeling the impotence of words.

"Well, for the thousandth time ... I'll become a superhuman parrot if I say it any more ... but for the thousandth time ... are you willing to live with me?"

Her head was lowered and chaos was in her heart. Her egotism—an anarchist infinitely disguised to itself—struggled against the drunkenness, the compressed pain and pleasure, which this man brought her.

"I think am, Joe."

"You're always thinking—do you ever decide anything?"

"Joe, you don't understand. If you're convinced I can make you happy, I'll live with you ... but are you sure?"

The question gave him a variant of grim amusement.

"Who in the devil's ever happy all the time ... or most of the time? That's a bed-time story for children. A man pays for his happiness with grief, and turmoil... back and forth all the time... or else he goes to sleep for the rest of his life. I don't mind paying, Alicia."

Abruptly, Alicia felt dwarfed and compliant.

"All right then, I'll live with you, Joe. That girl out there's worth ten of me, but if you want to take a chance..."

She kissed him and was mysterious to herself—the turbulence of emotions too complicated to be joy and far too disembodied to be sorrow. When she returned to the first living-room with Joe, they discovered—after a short search—that Anna had quietly slipped out of the apartment. Joe ran through the outer hallway and courtyard, hoping to spy or overtake her, but she had disappeared. Re-entering the living-room, he was morose.

"Damn it, I wish this hadn't happened. It's a rotten shame. She must have thought we were throwing a hint for her to leave."

"Joe, I'm just as sorry as you are, and that's the truth—" Alicia, pottering around the desk, tried hard to bring life to a sympathy which she did not quite feel.

Joe eyed her distrustfully.

"I wonder whether you meant that, kid."

"Of course I do."

Joe sat down and looked determinedly reflective.

"I'm going to phone her around noon, the minute I wake up. She's been hurt enough without getting any extra slaps."

Alicia, standing near him, raised her eyebrows with an impulsive irritation.

"I'm glad you're so remarkably solicitous about her."

"Why the sarcasm all of a sudden?"

"Because I'm not sure whether you don't care for her as much as you care for me... only in a different way."

"Certainly I care for her. She has an eighteen-karat mind, and if there's anything petty about her, I've never discovered it."

"Just a paragon in human form. I don't see how you can resist her."

"Alicia, have you any tolerance in your make-up?"

"Sometimes, but I can't understand one thing—you hardly ever praise me to my face, and you're always flinging bouquets at her. What do you see in me anyway?"

Joe had risen and was wandering around the room.

"I see a shaky, imperfect human, like myself . . . full of maybes and ranklings . . . grudges and weak spots . . . but trying just the same to be honest and clear. We have minds but we never use them two-thirds of the time, outside of the tricks we need to keep alive. I'm not good enough for Anna. I'm crazy to keep her as a friend. I love you because . . . oh, hell, because there is no because. You can spy something mighty fine in a human being, or mighty rotten, but that's only the skeleton. The flesh isn't there."

Alicia became humble, carried out of herself. She walked up to him, kissed him. They half reclined on a broad divan in the front of the room, and as he kissed her breasts, stroked her body, he was mystified, for a moment, by the unbelievable tumult in his heart. It was incredible but beautiful to be insane—the sane ones knew nothing of happiness. They could never quite abandon themselves, never rid themselves of quivers of caution, reticence. When they loved, it was either a wild, half-cruel and half-contrite lust—like the man and woman in a Hemingway novel—or it was respect plus a moderate amount of physical desire, but they were never insane . . . madly delicate to themselves and each other . . . hushed in the midst of their most intense contacts . . . unified and, whirlpoolish, far beyond brutal or sentimental motives.

The outside buzzer sounded repeatedly. Wrenching himself away from the purified dream, Joe felt that reality was never more than a senseless intrusion upon the innate fantasy of living. He walked to the door and opened it. Alicia heard profane words from a strange, rasping voice and then three shots, which sounded like steel cracking apart. For a moment she was paralyzed with fear. She could hear the sound of someone running down the hallway. She stood up and walked slowly to the door, feeling as though she were dragging a universe with each step. Joe had fallen to his haunches in the hallway and was holding himself up with one hand on the floor. Stains of blood were widening out on his shirt, just below the shoulder, and on one of his trouser-legs near the groin. His face was contorted and yet oddly peaceful. After Alicia had knelt beside him, he whispered to her:

"Call a police ambulance and keep cool, kid. I'm not going to croak... don't worry."

"Joe, tell me—who did it?"

"Sam Regatto... owns the speak' next to mine. He thinks I got him in bad with the cops... thinks I squealed on a couple of crooks selling hash' for him... but don't say a word to anyone. Promise me ... not a single word."

"I promise—" Alicia's eyes were glistening with tears.

All of life seemed to be a violent fraud now, a never-ending masquerade of ill-will, with naked moments, such as the present one, arriving when they were least expected. She looked up and saw people standing around her—the Negro elevator boy, men and women in hastily donned bath-robes and overcoats above pajamas—but they were all unreal to her. They seemed to be gruesome and comical. They made her laugh hysterically.

Chapter Four

CRANNYSIDE, in Queens, Long Island, was an area of houses spread over several blocks and grouped into a neighborhood-association. The buildings on each block stood separately, with small front lawns and long, wide inner gardens and play-grounds shared alike by all of the residents. The houses were all of reddish brown brick and two stories high, but the builders had made each one at least slightly different from the others. Some had flat roofs and others showed angular ones. Still others flaunted black, wooden eaves and gables. The irregularity continued in narrow and wider floor-spaces, open and closed porches, and the varied structures of windows and doorsteps. The idea had been to a void the dull, soulless monotony of houses exactly like each other, standing in precise rows and so often seen on the outskirts of New York City, and yet, in Crannyside, the alterations were mostly timid and minor. The effect was that of a person who had decided to be original and then checked himself after the first inch or two.

Bulletin boards stood on the corners, announcing the activities of the neighborhood, which included a Little Theatre group, a debating society, a contract-bridge club, and other clubs for parents and children. It was all serene, brightly industrious and well washed, on the surface. Guns were roaring in China and the bread-lines were still shuffling wearily forward in cities throughout America, but

Crannyside was determined to be peaceful and removed. Some of its inhabitants—minor artists and writers—even played with Communism during the more daring moments of their evening parties, but the prevailing motto was always the same—indignant words followed by cautious actions to safeguard the pocket-book. In Crannyside, the spirit of radicalism was little more than an eager tongue seeking to charm away the feeling of inward double-dealing and paralysis, yet even here the sham was clearly divided and the conservative residents looked down upon the talkative "radicals" and refused to mingle with them to the smallest extent.

On this particular morning, the day before Christmas, patches and streaks of snow were still on the ground, and the box-hedges, fronting some of the houses, raised their intricacies of bare branches and twigs, like a petrified tangle of fingers and wrists swaying slightly in the wind. The grass expanses were dry yellow with the faintest touches of green, and the saplings and young trees stood like rattling, patient expectancies, helpless and yet invincible. The sky was clear and the air mildly cold. At this hour, 8 A.M., people were beginning to trickle from the doorways, walking toward the subway station. Girls, some of them pretty, sped to their daily drudgery in offices—self-conscious and enclosed, with too much cosmetics on their faces and wearing fur-trimmed and all-fur coats, for which, in many cases, they had mortgaged the last drop of their hearts and souls. Business men and clerks swung along the pavement—always the immaculate front of black derbies, gray and brown felts, glistening shoes, tight and ugly ties and collars—and the sleepy faces of these men showed the inordinate strain of living in New York. They were stiffly set, hard around the eyes and often frowning to offset the feeling of over-worked unimportance.

These pilgrims to the subway walked quickly and ignored one

another, except for coolly measuring side-glances and occasional, clipped helloes—unless they happened to notice another member of their own, small and fixed, social groups. Here, as elsewhere in New York City, the spirit of camaraderie was scarcely more than a myth summoned to ease the conscience in the body of a relentless materialism.

In one of the rear houses, standing close to the Long Island Railroad tracks, Mona and Alicia were stirring in their beds, rubbing the sleep from their eyes. They had moved into the two-room flat almost a month before, to escape from the suspected espionage of detectives, and the telephone calls wherein strange voices admonished them to "keep their mouths shut, if they knew what was good for them." Mona knew a girl who lived in Crannyside, and through her services, they had sub-leased the already furnished apartment in which they now lived.

On the night of the shooting, and afterwards, Alicia had been frequently grilled and visited by detectives, but her obstinate silence, and the lack of evidence implicating her in any way, had finally induced these honest gentlemen to leave her in peace. According to their custom, they were always grimly assiduous in the case of a small shooting and curiously paralyzed, or inefficient, when ganglords shot and larger kidnappings and crimes were perpetrated.

Rising from the bed, Alicia walked into the other room and shook one of Mona's shoulders.

"Wake up, you sleepy-head. It's eight o'clock."

Mona, already half awake, squinted at Alicia with the far-off resentment of a child on her broad face. With the golden hair storming around her forehead, her neck, and one firm white breast peeping hugely from the lavender night-robe, she looked exactly like an overgrown child who had been thrashed and put to bed for some minor offense. Alicia pinched Mona's chin.

"Get up—do you hear me? It's after eight now."

"I don't care if it's after eighteen."

"You'll care all right, if you lose your job."

Mona became wide awake now. The child, born of sleep, departed and a residue of the old, protective worldliness, the instinctive girding against an imminent and distasteful day, stole back to her face.

"Nertz... you spoiled a perfectly wonderful dream. I was riding down the street on a pink elephant and people were clapping their hands and throwing roses at me, and I didn't have a stitch of anything on."

"Did you have a nice time with Stanley last night?"

"Hush up."

"I hope the roses didn't have thorns on them, since you weren't wearing anything."

"Oh, be quiet. You're too sly to tell me about your dreams. You know I'd kid the life out of you."

They scuffled good-naturedly, and then Mona rose from the bed.

Alicia had changed during the intervening weeks. Her eyes were less confident and seemed to be wondering whether there was much distinction between life's blows and caresses. Her face had found that wisdom which shrinks from its own emptiness. She had discovered that she could be inexcusably treacherous to herself and that her emotions could run amok at the smallest provocation. It was not neurasthenia—that unbalanced fight between visions of frustration and victory—but rather the admission that she was unhappy from causes beyond her comprehension, and that she must become wild in the hopeless effort to remedy the situation. What she did not know was that her mind could not keep pace with her feelings and that both sides were forever distressed by the discrepancy.

The alterations in Mona, on the other hand, were less perceptible and largely mental. Talking to Bingham and other men, and comparing their words with the remembered ones in Emil's conversation, she had commenced to notice differences previously invisible. The others had their little rows of ideas, fixed as stone, and bowed to them without undue questioning. In their less serious talk, they were usually kidding with a sexual undercurrent—or with kindness and malice peacefully inseparable—but otherwise they were intent upon mildly assailing and yet apologizing for the vicious, deceitful, material system in which they were caught. Emil was interested in exposing, while the others wanted to hide from themselves and life, and yet preserve a moderate air of investigation. Mona called it: "Spilling some of the beans but leaving most of them for supper." She still clung to Stanley because Emil seemed to be so unattainable—leagues removed—and Stanley was the best among the others whom she knew, but the longing for Emil was always lurking under her thoughts and beneath her conscious emotions.

As the girls bathed, dressed and groomed themselves, they kept up an intermittent conversation. Mona tried to be cheerful.

"Say, how's Joe feeling since he left the hospital?"

"Oh, he gets a little pain in his side now and then, but otherwise he seems to be all right."

"How are you two going to celebrate Christmas Eve?'"

"Celebrate, my aunt! I'm tired of drinking and dancing my feet off all the time. Joe'll be busy at his speak' and I don't want to sit there and watch him, so I've arranged to meet him at his flat about two in the morning."

"But what'll you do until then?"

"Sit here and read, like a little puss in the corner, and I suppose

I'll pinch myself every now and then, to see if I'm real."

A pause.

"You're happy with Joe now, aren't you?"

"I am not."

Another pause.

"Gee, but you are a difficult person, Alicia. What's the trouble *now*?"

Alicia sighed.

"Same old thing. I've promised to live with him and we've even got the day set, right after New Year's Eve, but . . ."

"Well?"

"Oh, he wants me to stop working and settle down with him, but I just can't do it. I wasn't cut out to be a nice, snoozey housewife, and I haven't brains enough to study anything. And then again, there's always Anna Stephens. He still sees her now and then—he's quite frank about it—but he tells me he doesn't have anything to do with her. It's supposed to be an intellectual companionship . . . and it burns me up, Mona."

Mona walked to Alicia and tapped one of her cheeks, and a darkening of pity and understanding was on Mona's face.

"I know, kid. You and Joe are always trying to boss each other because you're a couple of 'fraidy-cats. You're afraid to stand alone and yet you can't bear to be ruled by anything, but you were meant for each other just the same. You go ahead and live with him. You'll quarrel and make up a hundred times, but you can't help it. You've got to fight first and be happy afterwards—it's in the very marrow of your bones."

Alicia shook her head as she fastened the hooks in the upper side of her gray and purple dress.

"I'm not so sure. We can't wrangle and wriggle all of our lives.

If our love never brings any real peace, any real ... oh, I don't know ... beauty, I guess ... then we'll have to kill it some time."

Mona lapsed into silence as she straightened out her simple, black and yellow frock and fussed with her hair before the dressing-table near one of the front windows. She thought that she was a poor person to be handing out advice and prophecy to another woman, when, in her own life, the present and the future were so snarled, so frequently forced and profitless. She had arranged to meet Stanley on the coming night and attend with him an elaborate party in a pent-house along upper Fifth Avenue, and she viewed the prospect with pleasure and foreboding slipping in and out, in the ritual of a hunger often unwilling to recognize itself. The party would be another chance to become frivolous, impertinent, choosey, indulgent—all of the vagaries and contritions peculiar to the feminine sex, and even more peculiar to a woman thoroughly dissatisfied with herself—but the party would also be flooded with alcohol, and if she drank, she knew that she might pass into one of her blackly scornful moods, insult Bingham, and then stumble aimlessly out into the night. On the other hand, it was hard not to drink, with men pressing glasses on her from all sides, and with every temptation to become careless, divinely, colossally careless, and to forget, or deliciously minimize, the underlying heaviness in her heart.

She sighed and then tried to make her mind blank, as she walked from the house with Alicia. Mona was still working as a manicurist, now in a barber ship near One Hundred and Tenth Street and Central Park West. Alicia had secured a temporary job as a cashier in a cafeteria which did not open before half past nine in the morning because it was located in the office-building district of Lower Broadway.

While Mona was busy at the shop, her thoughts persisted in racing with her fingers. Would she ever see Emil again—that lovely, crippled, hedged-in son-of-a-gun? Oh, damn the moth-eaten pride, the silly—what was it?—the silly, shivery desire to hold her head above any man . . . which kept her from running to his abode and making everything plain to him. Muscles and health were precious things, certainly, but when they were not supported, or replaced, by mental attractions and beautiful emotions . . . something unique . . . apart from the obvious passions of the street, they became gradually tiresome, lacking in mysteries. In a respectable, well-mannered man they were often comical—the rooster trying so desperately not to strut—and among other men they were frequently abusive and conceited. Besides, Emil's body might be twisted but his skin was clear and his face well balanced. But he was beyond her reach. He wanted girls who were lunatics, dreamy, arty poseurs—the blind little fool.

Her thoughts travelled to Stanley. Now there was a man whose petty and larger sides were continually fighting against one another —a man stumbling here, getting a glimpse there. Stanley was conventional but he sought to laugh at it, to keep it from becoming too marked. Stanley was mercenary but he became ashamed of it, at times, and attempted to reach out toward what he called "higher things." Stanley saw the cruel, rotten system around him but he tried to slap it and pin a flower on it, at one and the same time. He couldn't look it straight in the face. Stanley was afraid to be different from other people, but he told himself that he was vastly different, to pat himself on the back. Stanley had all of the coarse emotions of the male, but he tried to keep them within "honorable bounds"—lie about their presence within him—and he had also just a bit of a dreamy ache, which bobbed up at unexpected moments. Poor Stan, he was so thoroughly human, and yet some spark, kindling mind and heart, simply wasn't there. If she ever married him, it would be because she wanted to fall asleep in the most convenient way and with a fair amount of physical enjoyment... for a while, anyway.

But the barber-shop blues were warbling—the old, babbling, bay-rum, male-drenched atmosphere—and she was manicuring the nails of a man who might leave her a half-dollar tip, because the holiday season was telling him to be generous. Funny, these people who really loosened up only at the end of each year. It was their great bandstand, grandstand opportunity to tell themselves that they were something which they were not—masterpieces of benevolence and good will. After January the second, they would troop into the barber shop again with their dimes, their occasional quarters. Well, on January the second she hoped that she wouldn't be in this shop, or any other. Manicuring was getting on her nerves. It involved so much blabbing to men: such a feigned interest in what they were saying, so many attempts to "date her up" and sometimes the surreptitious try at caressing her hands, pressing knees, while she was working. After the first of the year she was willing to be an office-worker, a switch-board operator—anything except manicuring!

She roused herself, realized that the fat man was speaking to her. He ran a haberdashery near the barber shop. He was half bald, with a carrot nose and almost middle-aged. He exuded a certain calculating affability.

"What's the trouble, Miss Farrideau—wearing your high hat today?"

"No, really. I'm awfully sorry. I was up late last night and I'm simply dead to the world. What were you saying?"

"I was asking you what kind of a Christmas you're going to have."

"Who, me? Oh, the same old thing. I'll get a few presents—mostly the things I don't need—and I'll get a little pie-eyed . . . not too much."

He looked at her, appreciatively. She wasn't a knockout but she was a pretty fair looker, and, as far as he knew, unmarried. He had just divorced his wife and had escaped with small alimony, and he was eager to celebrate his independence, to enjoy sex again without legal responsibilities.

"That's the stuff I like to hear, and I'm not kidding either. The way girls are drinking nowadays, it makes a man blush, honest. When a woman drinks too much she loses all of her charm and her beauty."

Mona felt like asking him whether the same rule applied to males, but she refrained.

"You're perfectly right. Every girl ought to know just how much she can hold."

"Absolutely. I read in the paper the other day where Mrs. Franklin D. Roosevelt said exactly the same thing."

As Mona polished and filed the nails, she laughed to herself at this joining of tolerant and respectable positions and she thought that liberal-minded people were much more humorous than hoboes, Communists or gangsters. The liberal-minded ones were always seeking to balance themselves between boredom and abandon, and congratulating themselves on the sensible feat, though it was a much easier one than being utterly repressed, or being without the slightest inhibition. The fat man resolved to test his chances with Mona.

"Of course, I know you must be dated up for Christmas Eve, but some friends of mine are staging a party tomorrow night. It's going to be a swell affair too. D'you think you could manage to come?"

As usual, Mona was tactfully evasive.

"I'd love to, really, but I've got another engagement. You drop in some time next week and maybe I'll have a night free."

"O.K. I'll do that little thing—" The fat man was dubious and yet mollified.

The remainder of the day was a minor ordeal to Mona—endless hands, expressive of everything from murder to gentleness, the badinage of the barbers and lulls in which she stretched herself and looked out at the familiar automobiles, shoddy store-fronts, lumbering street-cars and buses. The people strode past with an air of bustling importance, to lend size to their little, prosy errands and returns. No one except the children dared to be aimless, natural, skittish. Mona felt that, if being grown up meant that one had to be largely dignified and warily alert, she wished that she were ten years old. Always the pose of deliberate restraint and sanity—suppose a woman suddenly skipped down a crowded street, because she was happy, or practiced a fox-trot while she was waiting for a subway train, or played tag with her boy-friend on the corner of Broadway and Forty-second—wouldn't that be *dreadful*?

At the end of the day she was tired and yet a bit more hopeful. Merkletrauer, the boss—a small man with a pigeon's face—gave her a five-dollar Christmas bonus and a kiss which landed on one of her eyes, as she ducked to avoid the attempt to reach her mouth, and the three other barbers, laughing inordinately, hung a piece of mistletoe over the bathroom door and vainly tried to snare her into passing beneath it. They were entirely without lust and they wanted to be gleefully boyish, to forget their stiff feet and strained eyes, and Mona kissed them all good night, and they called her a good skate, and sipped a little wine together before they parted with the traditional "Merry Christmas!"

When Mona returned to Crannyside she found a note from Alicia stating that Alicia had departed to attend a Broadway show and might not reappear until the following afternoon. Mona smiled—"sit here and read, like a little puss in the corner"—that kid would have to be handcuffed and roped down first! Alicia's mind wasn't stupid, Mona thought, but three-fourths of the time, the fever in her bones was rocking it to sleep. Mona slept for over two hours and then, waking up, felt chipper and girded—the magic reserve energy still in her youth. When Stanley rang and entered the apartment, she was still in the midst of dressing and, after a hasty kiss, he waited for her in the front room. They spoke back and forth, through the half-drawn, yellow portières, and then she walked out, clad in a long, violet and mauve evening gown, with slippers to match—an outfit which had devoured the last penny of her savings. Stanley had purchased two lavender orchids for her, and as he pinned them just below her left shoulder-strap, he kissed her hair, her neck and the upper part of her bosom. He was wearing a full-dress suit with a white rose-bud on the lapel. His blunt-jawed face was tenderly complacent, with a touch of nervous deference. At bottom, he was skeptical of his happiness. In his disposal, women were unreliable, often unwittingly cruel, unless they had a permanently frenzied and prostrate desire for a man, and in that case they became dull and pitiful. He thought that most successful unions, married or otherwise, were those in which the man and woman committed very occasional infidelities, with a mutual knowledge and tolerance, or flirted just enough to give birth to a doubt, to rouse the dormant jealousy. Without such tactics and attitudes, he believed that the attachments were bound to end in quarrels, in veiled boredoms or endurance tests.

During the intervening weeks Mona had become a goad and a delight, impalpably mixed. She had given him submissions, refusals, disparagements and praise, in an always unexpected rotation, and he had interpreted the entire procedure as partly a battle against her own growing affection and, in the other part, her desire to keep him on edge and thus avoid losing him. It was all typically, deliriously feminine and a man never knew what the outcome would be, but, he sentimentalized, she must be caring for him more and more, since she still continued to give him the unsteadying sweetness of her embraces at irregular intervals.

He fumbled in one of his pockets now and drew out a small black case, opening and extending it to her.

"Here's the Christmas gift, kid—" His voice was shaky, almost abashed. The case contained a jade and turquoise necklace, with the stones exquisitely matched, and it had cost him a considerable sum. She held it in her hands, admiringly.

"Oh, thanks, Stan, thanks ever so much. You're a perfect *dear*. Why, it's one of the loveliest, loveliest things I've ever seen."

She kissed him, quickly.

"If you think they're Woolworth stones, just have them tested some time—" He was revelling in a material importance, trying hard to joke itself out of existence.

"Don't be numb. I know it's real but I don't care how much you paid for it. It really is beautiful."

Beneath her pleasure she was sorry that the pleasure was not deeper, that she could not fly into a prolonged rhapsody over his gifts and become the hearty comrade, sheering into loyally adoring attendant, he craved. Somehow presents of necklaces, furs, topaz earrings, dropped into her heart and disappeared, like stones thrown into a bottomless well, and her gratitude was only an intense effort to pretend that they meant something to her. Her vanity had changed—it was scarcely more than a nicely tingling habit now, derided by the starved unrest in her heart, the poorly equipped curiosities in her mind.

She told herself that she knew, in general, every word and action that would be exchanged between Stanley and herself until the coming dawn, and the absence of anticipation depressed her. Perhaps she would not see him again after this night . . . return all of the poor boy's presents . . . but, it was all so involved. His gifts, his spontaneous gallantries, brought her an uncomfortable sense of obligation, and the touch of his body was a mild but definite opiate. The defeatist side of her nature urged her to accept him, to laugh at her unhappiness so steadily and effectively that the laughter would finally become real, and the unhappiness would vanish, substantially and to most of her consciousness, and she would find herself a babbling housewife tied to an endurable man and immersed in a routine of small, concrete tasks and pleasures.

She was sitting beside Stanley, on a brown plush settee between the windows of the front room. She still held the necklace in her hands. Stanley was glowing with certainty and pride.

"Are you going to wear it tonight?"

"No, I don't think so. It doesn't match the dress I have on."

She rose and deposited the necklace in her bureau in the rear room, after which she returned to the settee. Stanley was humming a popular tune and beating the time with his feet—pleased with himself and the world.

"It's going to be a great party tonight. The boss ordered five cases of champagne yesterday, and he's rigged up a miniature bar right beside the dance floor. Of course, it seems a shame to spend so much money in these lousy times, with people standing in breadlines all over . . . but Christ, the old boy gave a couple of thou' to that Newspaper Basket Fund too . . . helped smear over his conscience, I guess."

"Oh, I wish I didn't have to go. I don't feel like parties."

He looked at her with surprise.

"Why, kid . . . what's the trouble? Aren't you feeling well?"

"Oh, there's nothing the matter with my health, but I'm blah just the same. Nothing seems to interest me any more."

He thought that she was merely weary of working almost every day and living in a cramped flat, and he was tenderly solicitous, as he held one of her hands.

"Listen, kid . . . you're a fool to keep on slaving in barber shops, handling the paws of a lot of bluffing muts. You can't do it all your life . . . and you might as well drop it now."

She shook her head.

"If it wasn't that, it would be something else just as tiresome. I've got to stand on my own feet . . . it's in my blood and I can't help it, unless . . ."

"Unless what?"

"Unless I really love a man."

"I suppose you're going to tell me you don't love me."

"I'm afraid I don't, Stan."

The silence was like the sudden lift of a knife from the deceptive sheath which had concealed it. The snug elation within Stanley died hard, saw the approach of dejection and closed his eyes feebly.

The door-bell rang and Mona answered it. Emil stumped into the room, breathing quickly from his climb up the stairway. He was dressed in a gray suit, with a soft blue collar and tie, and minus an overcoat, despite the weather. His cheeks had red spots on them, from walking in the cold wind, and his face, with its tight mouth and brown eyes, was expressive of his character—timid and bold in a subtle fusion of which he was unaware, and relatively fearless toward all matters except his own treacherously recurring self-despairs.

In the midst of her surprise, all of the complexities and resistances vanished within Mona and she became, in scarcely more than a second, comparatively simple, girlish and once more brightly necessary to herself.

"Why, *Emil* . . . you're the last person I expected to see. What gave you the impulse and . . . and how did you find out where I lived?"

Emil smiled, diffidently.

"Well, you see . . . my parents moved recently—they're living only a few blocks away from here now. I ran into a girl-friend of yours a couple of days ago and she gave me your address. Her name's Rea Johnson."

"Rea. Oh, sure . . . I used to work in the same place with her."

Emil looked at Bingham, uncertainly.

"I had supper with my folks tonight and then I decided to drop in on you . . . just to say hello to you. I'll be going in a minute."

"You will not—you'll stay right here—" Mona had a caressing, motherly, vibrant inflection in her voice.

After she had introduced Emil to Bingham, the conversation was one of forced amenities interrupted by hesitant, woefully pregnant silences. Stanley had been taken aback, at first, by the joyous welcome bestowed on Emil, but his jealousy had been almost instantly swallowed by an easily ordered pity. The poor, crippled kid—Mona sympathized with him, had a certain degree of compassionate friendliness toward him, but it couldn't be more than that. She was too essentially normal and straight in her physical tastes. A civilized man accepted such deviations, instead of bristling up within himself whenever his woman seemed to be in any way interested in another man.

Emil, on the other hand, felt nervous and out of place. In spite of his longing to remain, he told himself that it would be an inevitably graceful act to leave, but he was tired from his long walk and prompted by an instinct which he could not define—a timorous, laughed-at expectation, persisting against all of the contrary evidence. Bingham was only a casual, conventional, fleshly figure to Emil—a pleasant-mannered correctly attired figure from the careful, evasive, material world, which always gave Emil the sensation of peering through a window, accidentally, before he walked off to his unworldly loneliness. Bingham rose from the settee.

"It's getting rather late. Don't you think we'd better be going, dear?"

Mona had been sitting with dread and indecision in her heart, beneath the compulsory smiles and patter—the social fortitude which was rule number one in civilization's etiquette book until liquor, carnal frenzy or outraged vanity blurred the print. She began almost to imagine that chance was plotting against her. First, her own self-loving, fearful blindness had spoiled a beautiful time with him, she thought, and then the kid, with a natural pride, had repulsed her when she had approached him at his newsstand and she had tried, like a fool, to be repentant without showing too much of it. After this she had run into the stifled, quarrelsome joke at "George's Rendezvous" . . . that pair of women, outlandishly dressed, "wild" in their talk and crazy or inspired, she didn't know which . . . and now she was once more trapped, on the verge of leaving him. They might become finally separated after this night—lost to each other in the hurried distractions and exhaustions of a huge city, since, with Alicia about to live with Joe, the present apartment would have to be relinquished after the first of the year. Again, if she asked Emil to visit her on some other night, he might mistake the invitation for a polite retreat and remain away—his pride and hers ... always the damn' stone wall of pride.

A ruthless impulse drove everything else out of her heart, as she deserted the chair and walked half way toward Bingham.

"I'm not going with you, Stan. I know it's horribly rude ... but I can't. I just can't. I've got to be alone with Emil and have a talk with him."

Emil stood up—distressed and trying to be sacrificial in the youthful desire "to be a gentleman," to make smoothly disclaiming postures over pain, direct complaint—though he laughed at both the desire and the phrase, very secretly and lightly, to himself.

"Please don't bother on my account, Mona. I'll drop in some other time."

Mona frowned at him.

"Yes, I know ... it's always some other time with us, but it's going to be different this time."

She turned to Bingham.

"I might as well tell you now, Stan—I'm in love with this kid here, just crazy in love with him. This is the first chance we've had to be alone together in months, and oh ... I can't help it, Stan. I've just got to stay here with him. I know it'll hurt you, but I've *got* to stay with him."

At first Bingham had been wrathfully stunned, but now a coldness mastered him and it was artificially conjured to save his pride—the old, gauche desire to strike a man, the impossibility of gratifying the desire at the expense of a cripple, the sneering effort to pretend an indifference and then compel it to become real—all of the self-elusive, clear and cloudy mixture of emotion meeting a sharply unwelcomed surprise. Women were innately treacherous, he thought. When they were not lying outright, they bribed a man with fractional promises, smiles, half-submissions, or else they were disagreeably, familiarly prostrate. It was his cue to become dead drunk on this night and attempt to seduce any girl who could be made sufficiently drunk herself—Why not? He knew that he would falter in carrying out such a plan—that an actual libertine was a man capable of being consistently deliberate and self-mean in his sexual tactics and, therefore, a man rarely in existence—but the assertion of it partly soothed his anger. During his sober periods, one of the items in his code was to remain outwardly unruffled in the face of an unexpected rejection—the droll, Anglo-Saxon version of "playing cricket"—no matter how venomous or agitated he might feel underneath it. Except for the suspicion of a sneer, his face was blank and his silence unbroken until he stood beside the door, his coat and hat in his hands. Then he smiled politely, with a perceptible effort, and spoke.

"Try not to be so abrupt the next time, Mona. You might have bad luck and run across a man who was . . . just a little violent. I think you understand what I mean."

As she looked at him a trace of tenderness, enlarged a bit by the secret feeling of guilt, crept through Mona's heart. She walked up to him. "Won't you kiss me good-bye . . . won't you realize I can't help myself?"

His smile became nastily fixed.

"No, I think I've done enough senseless things without this one."

He opened the door and walked swiftly out, ignoring Mona's soft *"Auf Wiedersehen*, Stan."

Emil was still perched on the settee, and he felt a troubled and mournful compulsion toward this man stepping out into the night

—felt that life was too often an unscrupulous battle royal, where the shrewd ones escaped most of the injury and the trusting ones were forever kicked and slapped. Yet, who could avoid being deeply hurt, from time to time? It was the eternal confusion of earth, in which one person's possessive desire collided with another person's failure to respond.

After closing the door, Mona stepped to one of the windows and watched Bingham, as he entered his machine and sped down the street. She tried intensely to feel sad, to acknowledge the sense of guilt, but the lightness in her heart was too relieved, too magically new to itself. Walking from the window she thought, suddenly, of the necklace.

"I'll have to mail it back to him Tuesday—" her voice was mechanical.

She turned and looked at Emil. Her face was loose, inhumanly buoyant. In spite of all that they wanted to say, these two long-separated people felt that every word could be condensed and amplified in the long-deferred sense of touch. Whether they remained together for months, years—whatever the time might be—they would be invisibly controlled and marked for the rest of their lives, beyond the over-rated urge of physical proximity. Mona cuddled Emil to her lap, on the settee, as though he were a falsely twisted baby, and the touch of her thighs, her breasts, could give him the reality of a straight body beyond any mere vision of sentimentality. Kissing Mona, Emil had the feeling of wings raising his mouth and hers to incalculable flight, lack of weight, and during lulls in the kissing, he thought that romance and sentimentality became an inevitable softness of hope necessary to prevent life from being too flat and prearranged, far outside of the self-insincere sugars and the grimly unquestioning realities facing each other in life.

The door opened and Alicia entered the apartment. Her hair was disordered; her black felt hat was crushed in one hand; and her face was stiff and frozen-eyed, as though it were staring at a nightmare and attempting, with the sheer refusal of eyes, to drive it out of existence. Mona jumped from the settee and hurried to Alicia.

"Alicia... darling... what's the matter... what's happened?"

Alicia closed her eyes and leaned against the wall beside the door. Her voice was hard, cracking apart.

"Joe killed himself."

"What!"

"Yes, he killed himself. I got in with my latch-key and... there he was sprawled out on the couch. He left a note saying he knew Regatto would get him, sooner or later, and he didn't want to live because... because we couldn't be happy together."

Alicia burst into weeping and Mona, weeping a bit herself, dragged Alicia into the back room, helped her to recline on the couch and strove, brokenly, to comfort her. As Emil listened to the weeping, the little, stifled words of sympathy, he was burdened with dark reflections. Life, especially in New York City, was a madness trying in every devious way to appear sane and practical and reasonably happy—a hurried, overwhelming cruelty in thousands of masquerades, briefly contented lulls, false snorings, and self-conscious repentances.

He closed his eyes and fell asleep on the settee.

THE END

www.ingramcontent.com/pod-product-compliance
Lightning Source LLC
La Vergne TN
LVHW031606060526
838201LV00063B/4750